Y0-CPD-069

$5.00

LANGSTON HUGHES

Joe Nazel

MELROSE SQUARE PUBLISHING COMPANY
LOS ANGELES, CALIFORNIA

JOE NAZEL is America's most prolific African-American writer, as the author of more than forty books, including both fiction and non-fiction. His contributions to Melrose Square's Black American Series include biographies of *Martin Luther King, Jr.*, and *Thurgood Marshall*. Educated in Ethnic Studies at the University of Southern California, he currently teaches and writes in Los Angeles.

To:

Charlotte and LeRoy, Joye, Reggie, Jubei, Sugiko,
Sheryl and Toi, Betty, Mary, Ron and Alyn,
Robin and Little Herman, John and Little John.

www.hollowayhousebooks.com

Consulting Editors for Melrose Square
Raymond Friday Locke
James Neyland

Originally published by Melrose Square, Los Angeles.
© 1994 by Holloway House.

This edition reprinted 2004

All rights reserved under International and Pan-American Copyright Conventions. No part of this book may be reproduced in any form or by electronic or mechanical means including information storage and retrieval systems without permission in writing from the publisher, except by a reviewer who may quote brief passages in a review. Published in the United States by Melrose Square Publishing Company, an imprint of Holloway House Publishing Company, 8060 Melrose Avenue, Los Angeles, California 90046. © 1994 by Joe Nazel..

Cover Painting: by Gerry Haylock, Allied Artists
Cover Design: by Bill Skurski

ISBN 0-87067-937-6

LANGSTON HUGHES

MELROSE SQUARE
BLACK AMERICAN SERIES

ELLA FITZGERALD
singer
NAT TURNER
slave revolt leader
PAUL ROBESON
singer and actor
JACKIE ROBINSON
baseball great
LOUIS ARMSTRONG
musician
SCOTT JOPLIN
composer
MATTHEW HENSON
explorer
MALCOLM X
militant black leader
CHESTER HIMES
author
SOJOURNER TRUTH
antislavery activist
BILLIE HOLIDAY
singer
RICHARD WRIGHT
writer
ALTHEA GIBSON
tennis champion
JAMES BALDWIN
author
JESSE OWENS
olympics star
MARCUS GARVEY
black nationalist leader
SIDNEY POITIER
actor
WILMA RUDOLPH
track star
MUHAMMAD ALI
boxing champion
FREDERICK DOUGLASS
patriot & activist
MARTIN LUTHER KING, JR.
civil rights leader
ZORA NEALE HURSTON
author
SARAH VAUGHAN
singer
LANGSTON HUGHES
poet

HARRY BELAFONTE
singer & actor
JOE LOUIS
boxing champion
MAHALIA JACKSON
gospel singer
BOOKER T. WASHINGTON
educator
NAT KING COLE
singer & pianist
GEORGE W. CARVER
scientist & educator
WILLIE MAYS
baseball player
LENA HORNE
singer & actress
DUKE ELLINGTON
jazz musician
BARBARA JORDAN
congresswoman
GORDON PARKS
photographer & director
MADAME C.J. WALKER
entrepreneur
MARY MCLEOD BETHUNE
educator
THURGOOD MARSHALL
supreme court justice
KATHERINE DUNHAM
dancer & choreographer
ELIJAH MUHAMMAD
relilgious leader
ARTHUR ASHE
tennis champion
A. PHILIP RANDOLPH
union leader
W.E.B. DU BOIS
scholar & activist
DIZZY GILLESPIE
musician & bandleader
COUNT BASIE
musician & bandleader
HENRY AARON
baseball player
MEDGAR EVERS
social activist
RAY CHARLES
singer & musician

CONTENTS

Chapter One

The
Color Line

THE MAN WHO would become known as the "poet laureate of black America" was born James Mercer Langston Hughes on February 1, 1902, in Joplin, Missouri. While he was still a very young man, the future poet dropped his first two names, opting for "Langston Hughes" as the public name that would gain international attention.

Hughes was born when the twentieth century was still new and America was still reeling from the assassination of President William McKinley in 1901. The colorful Theodore Roosevelt had succeeded to the

Langston Hughes, the "poet laureate of black America," became one of the most important poets and playwrights of the flowering of African-American arts known as the "Harlem Renaissance."

nation's highest office; and, the year after Hughes' birth, brothers Orville and Wilbur Wright fulfilled mankind's long-standing dream of flight in the then obscure town of Kitty Hawk, North Carolina.

The dawning of the twentieth century offered a sense of hope and prosperity for most Americans, but Langston Hughes would quickly discover that he and other African Americans were excluded from the "American Dream" by a formidable and oppressive color line. Hughes learned young, like other black children throughout America, that education and career opportunities would continue to be dictated by skin color.

In 1903, W.E.B. Du Bois, one of the most vocal African Americans committed to the struggle against racism, observed in his most popular book, *The Souls of Black Folk*, "The problem of the twentieth century is the problem of the color line—the relation of the darker to the lighter races of men in Asia and Africa, in America and the islands of the sea."

Due to his scholarly writings, W.E.B. Du Bois was one of the most powerful and influential activists against anti-Negro violence and racial discrimination to gain national and international attention. He was born in 1868, the year that the Fourteenth Amendment granted citizenship rights to "all persons born

During Langston Hughes' youth, the most influential African-American spokesman was W.E.B. Du Bois, founder of The Crisis *magazine, the official voice of the National Association for the Advancement of Colored People.*

or naturalized in the United States" and guaranteed equal protection under the law. Du Bois soon learned that the rights supposedly "guaranteed" by the Constitution to all men, were more often than not denied to African Americans because of their race.

Du Bois graduated from "historically black" Fisk University and later became one of the first African Americans to be granted a doctorate from prestigious Harvard University in 1895. His determination to fight racism prompted Du Bois to call a meeting of twenty-nine African-American professionals, teachers, and editors to address the problems facing African Americans. The group, including newspaper editors Monroe Trotter and J. Max Barber and college professor John Hope, met in July of 1905 and founded the Niagara Movement "to organize thoroughly the intelligent and honest Negroes throughout the United States for the purpose of insisting on manhood rights, industrial opportunity, and spiritual freedom."

In 1906, as head of the Niagara Movement, Du Bois escalated the struggle for full human rights for African Americans and issued his now famous, "Address to the Country," which read in part: "We will not be satisfied to take one jot or title less than our full manhood rights. We claim for ourselves every single right that belongs to a freeborn American, political, civil, and social; and until we get these rights we will never cease to protest and assail the ears of America. The battle we wage is not for ourselves alone but for all true Americans."

The Niagara Movement was ineffective in its battle against white-on-black violence. In 1906, riots rocked Atlanta, Georgia. A white mob attacked African Americans and looted and burned the property. When the rioting ended seventy African Americans had been injured and twelve killed. For African Americans there was no "equal protection under law."

Langston Hughes was only six years old when, in August of 1908, a race riot exploded in Springfield, Illinois. The violence, which erupted near the home of President Abraham Lincoln, the Great Emancipator, was just one of a series of racial confrontations that rocked every corner of the nation. A "separate but equal" doctrine not only divided the races but also assigned an inferior status to African Americans based solely on race. The separatist doctrine was brutally enforced as whites used violence to deny blacks jobs and housing both in the North and in the South.

Du Bois wasn't alone in the struggle to end discrimination against African Americans. As the violence escalated, well-meaning whites, horrified by the rising number of lynchings and other outrages, stepped forward in hopes of organizing in order to bring an end to the oppression.

In 1909, the year after the tragic riot in Springfield, Illinois, white liberal activist Mary White Ovington called for a meeting of liberal whites and African-American intellectual and religious leaders, among them the noted W.E.B. Du Bois.

White liberals William English Walling, Dr. Henry Moskowitz, and Oswald Garrison Villard attended the meeting. Walling had called for national support for African Americans in an article for the Springfield *Independent*.

Du Bois headed the group, which included Jane Addams, Francis J. Grimke, John Dewey, Ida Wells Barnett, John Haynes Holmes, Bishop Alexander Walters, and William Dean Howells.

The outcome of the historic meeting of white and black Americans was the founding of the National Association for the Advancement of Colored People. In a 1910 editorial in the NAACP's newly established print voice, *The Crisis,* founded and edited by Du Bois, the NAACP's platform was outlined and the war against racism declared. The NAACP, read the

Ida B. Wells Barnett was among the group of black and white leaders who joined together in 1909 to form the NAACP to wage war against the virulent racism that was on the rise in the United States in the early decades of the century.

editorial, "stands for the rights of men, irrespective of color or race, for the highest ideals of American democracy, and for reasonable but earnest and persistent attempts to gain these rights and realize these ideals."

Du Bois' writings had a powerful influence over Langston, especially during his formative years as a pre-teen. Du Bois' was a strong voice speaking out on behalf of African Americans, a voice that helped shape Langston's approach to his art. "All art is propaganda," wrote Du Bois, "and ever must be, despite the wailing of the purists. I stand in utter shamelessness and say that whatever art I have for writing has been used always for propaganda for gaining the right of black folk to love and enjoy. I do not care a damn for any art that is not used for propaganda. But I do care when propaganda is confined to one side while the other is stripped and silent."

Hughes would write, at the height of his career, "I have...often been termed a propaganda or protest writer.... That designation has probably grown out of the fact that I write about what I know best, and being a Negro in this country is tied up with difficulties that cause one to protest naturally."

By birthright, it seemed, young Langston Hughes would be faced with a life of struggle, rejection, and more struggle, as he came of age

Mary White Ovington was one of the most important of the white liberal activists who helped to organize the NAACP, and she continued to serve on its board for the rest of her life.

in an America that would not, in his lifetime, resolve the "problem of the color line."

James N. Hughes, Langston's father, was an educated and ambitious man. He yearned for much more out of life than racial conditions in America would allow him to achieve. When Langston was still a child, his parents separated and his father sought a brighter future in Mexico, beyond the restrictions of the color line.

Langston's mother, Carrie Mercer Langston Hughes, was also well educated. But there were few jobs available to her that would allow her to make use of her skills and education. Hughes and his mother were forced to move from city to city as she searched for employment. Though James Hughes prospered in Mexico, his mother, an educated woman, found it difficult to attain meaningful employment in her home country.

Langston's parents made one attempt at reconciliation, and he, his mother, and his grandmother joined his father in Mexico City. The language barrier and a major earthquake that struck Mexico City while they were there convinced Carrie that her family would be better off in Kansas, and they returned to the United States without his father.

As his mother moved from place to place in search of employment, the young Langston

Oswald Garrison Villard served as chairman of the board of the NAACP for many years until he and W.E.B. Du Bois came to a strong disagreement that resulted in Villard's resignation.

was often shunted from one relative to another. He lived and attended school in seven cities throughout the Midwest before graduating from high school, including Lawrence, Kansas; Topeka, Kansas; Lincoln, Illinois; and Cleveland, Ohio.

Too often, Langston was forced to change schools and move in with yet another relative just as he had made new friends, which was one of the most unsettling aspects of his school years.

In an essay entitled, "Ten Thousand Beds," Hughes would recall the sudden moves that kept him rootless. "I figure I have slept in at least ten thousand beds," mused Hughes. "As a child I was often boarded out, sent to stay with relatives, foster-relatives, or friends of the family..., so quite early in life I got used to a variety of beds from the deep feather beds of the country to the studio couches of the town, from camp cots to my uncle's barber chair in Kansas City elongated to accommodate me."

Life was difficult for young Langston and his mother. Her income could only provide a meager existence. Hughes recalls in *The Big Sea*, the first volume of his two-volume autobiography, that he often scoured the city's alleys for old wooden boxes and crates that he and his mother might burn in their small stove

It was rare that Langston was able to live with his mother, Carrie Hughes because she was constantly moving from place to place to find work. When it was possible Langston moved with her; when it was not, he lived with other relatives.

to keep warm.

There were good times, too. When living with his mother in Topeka, Kansas, young Langston was first introduced to the theater. His mother would take him to as many plays as she could afford, including *Buster Brown, Under Two Flags, Uncle Tom's Cabin,* and the classic opera *Faust.*

Langston was intrigued by the live performances and the powerful emotions they stirred within him. Too, they helped him and his mother to escape, though momentarily, from their financial troubles. But even then, Langston was not considering the theater or writing as career options.

Langston was an eager student, and his mother encouraged him to study and excel. She insisted that he get the best education available to blacks at the time, going as far as to force a nearby all-white Harrison Street School to enroll him. Once enrolled, Langston had little trouble with students or teachers.

One of the most important family figures in Langston's early years was his grandmother in Lawrence, Kansas. Mrs. Mary Sampson Patterson Langston was a proud woman who was not known to "beg or borrow." She was a strong black woman who refused to work as a maid in white homes or as a cook in white kitchens no matter how hard it might be to find dignified employment. She was also an educated woman, a graduate of Oberlin College, and well-versed on the history of African Americans.

Hughes described his grandmother as "looking very much like an Indian: copper-colored, with long black hair, just a little gray in places at age seventy. Hughes was in the second grade when his mother was forced to make one of her moves to another city to take a job. He was sent to live with his grandmother until his mother could afford to send for him.

Though he loved his grandmother and enjoyed the quality time she spent with him reading from the Bible and from black periodicals like *The Crisis* magazine, Langston was lonely. He turned to books to fill the long hours away from his mother.

Chapter Two

In Grandma's Hands

LIVING WITH HIS grandmother in Lawrence, Kansas, was a learning experience for young Langston Hughes. In many ways, she helped to shape his future outlook on life and on his work. It was virtually at his grandmother's knee, as she sat reading aloud to him from black magazines and newspapers like Robert S. Abbott's popular *Chicago Defender*, that young Langston was exposed to parts of American history that were not available in most American schools—the vibrant history of African Americans.

His grandmother told him exciting stories of

Perhaps the longest period of stability for young Langston was the period when he lived with his grandmother, Mary Langston, who told him stories that fired his imagination.

heroic African-American men and women who had devoted—and were devoting—their very lives to the struggle for complete freedom for their race. The stories provided young Langston with positive role models, preparing him for the racism he would face throughout his life.

From the very beginning of American history, African peoples, the ancestors of today's African Americans, had a major impact on the birth, growth, and development of the emerging nation and its culture.

One of these was Crispus Attucks, who was the first man to fall in America's fight for independence from England. He was killed on a wintry night in March of 1770 as he led patriots, black and white, against armed British soldiers. Over a century later, poet John Boyle O'Reilly would commemorate the historic night, writing: "And honor to Crispus Attucks, who was leader and voice that day: The first to defy, and the first to die...."

There was also Frederick Douglass, former slave who took his freedom by standing up to and fighting a "slave-breaker" hired to beat the thirst for freedom from so-called "uncooperative" slaves. Once free, Douglass became a full-time abolitionist, dedicated to the complete abolition of slavery in America.

In an historic speech, given in Rochester,

As a child, Langston heard of the heroic efforts of Frederick Douglass in securing his freedom and then becoming one of the most important leaders of the abolition movement to end the institution of slavery in the United States.

New York, on July 5, 1852, Douglass attacked slavery in America in brilliant oratory, saying: "In the solitude of my spirit I see clouds of dust raised on the highways of the South.... I hear the doleful wail of fettered humanity on the way to the slave-markets, where the victims are to be sold like horses, sheep and swine.... There I see the tenderest ties ruthlessly broken, to gratify the lust, caprice, and rapacity of the buyers and sellers of men. My soul sickens at the sight."

Langston's grandmother told him of the heroic exploits of Harriet Tubman, an African American who was a Union spy during the Civil War as well as an "engineer" on the famed Underground Railroad. Young Langston listened eagerly, quietly visualizing this strong, courageous African-American woman who had led scores of escaped slaves to safety and freedom in the North and in Canada.

She told him about her own first husband, Sheridan Leary, who had believed so strongly in freedom for all people that he had fought and died at the side of abolitionist John Brown at Harper's Ferry, Virginia. The unsuccessful raid, which would eventually cost John Brown his life, was in reaction to a ruling by U.S. Supreme Court Chief Justice Roger B. Taney that "a Negro has no rights which a white man need respect."

*Langston's grandmother's first husband had been Sheridan
Leary, a follower of John Brown who had died in the famous
raid at Harper's Ferry, Virginia, intended to be the beginning of
a massive slave revolt throughout the South.*

The statement was part of a decision in a Supreme Court case *Dred Scott v. Sanford,* in which slave Dred Scott sought his freedom through legal recourse, on the grounds that his "master" had taken him into "free" territory, where slavery was illegal. Scott believed that he should have become free during the time he and his owner lived in the northern state.

But the ruling of the U.S. Supreme Court declared that African Americans, slave or free, were not, in fact, citizens of the United States and therefore had no rights.

In 1858, John Brown held an anti-slavery meeting at Catham, Canada, where he condemned slavery and the brutal treatment of black free men and women in America. He spoke before a small gathering of twelve whites and thirty-four blacks. Then, on October 16, 1859, he made a decisive and courageous step toward ending the vicious slave tradition. Brown, leading thirteen whites and five blacks, attacked the federal arsenal at Harper's Ferry, Virginia. Brown's goal was to secure arms and ammunition that might be used to combat Virginia slaveowners in a war to end slavery.

"I pity the poor in bondage that have none to help them," Brown was quoted in the *New York Herald;* "that is why I am here; not to gratify any personal animosity, revenge, or vindictive spirit.... You may dispose of me easily, but this question is still to be settled—the Negro question—the end is not yet."

Brown's fearless group held the arsenal, though under heavy siege from federal troops, for two days. A black man, Dangerfield Newby, was the first of Brown's small band of men to be killed in the furious battle. Newby, though free, had a wife and seven children in slavery only thirty miles from Harper's Ferry.

Sheridan Leary, Hughes' maternal grandmother's first husband, and two of Brown's own sons were also killed in the fighting. One black freedom fighter did manage to escape capture and find his way to freedom.

The futile assault on Harper's Ferry gained national attention. Whites feared an all-out uprising among free black men and slaves. For weeks after the assault the newspapers kept the story alive. Most whites looked upon Brown's actions as treasonous.

Blacks, slave and free, and abolitionists throughout the world sought to remember John Brown and honor him as described by Frederick Douglass (who had advance knowledge of the raid) as "the noble old hero whose one right hand has shaken the foundation of the American Union."

John Brown was tried in court, convicted of

General Robert E. Lee led the United States troops in defeating John Brown at Harper's Ferry. Most of Brown's followers, among them his own sons and a number of slaves and free

blacks, were killed in the fight, which took place at the United States aresenal. Brown himself was captured and hanged. However, his actions did much to precipitate the Civil War.

treason, and sentenced to be executed for his part in planning and leading the raid on Harper's Ferry. In his last moments Brown boldly declared, "Now, if it is deemed necessary that I should forfeit life for the furtherance of the ends of justice, and mingle my blood further with the blood of my children and with the blood of millions in this slave country whose rights are disregarded by wicked, cruel, and unjust enactments, I say, let it be done."

On December 2, 1859, John Brown was hanged. *The Weekly Anglo-African* newspaper, in New York, quoted a Reverend Farnett who declared, "The day has come in which the nation is about to suffer a great crime to be perpetrated against the cause of liberty. Today John Brown is to offer up his life, a sacrifice for the sake of justice and equal human rights. Henceforth the second day of December will be called 'Martyr's Day.'... The withered hand of an old man whose hairs are white with the frosts of nearly seventy winters has given the death blow to American slavery.... Hero, martyr, farewell."

That John Wilkes Booth was in Harper's Ferry and observed the hanging is an interesting historical footnote.

John Copeland and Shields Green, African Americans who fought at John Brown's side, were also sentenced to be executed for participating in the raid. On December 16, 1859, both Copeland and Green were hanged.

Almost a half-century after the famed assault on Harper's Ferry, President Theodore Roosevelt honored Grandma Mary as the last surviving widow of John Brown's courageous freedom fighters. Until that time her only memento from her husband's daring feat was his bullet-riddled clothing.

On January 1, 1863, while the Civil War bloodied American soil, North and South, President Abraham Lincoln ordered an end to the tragic tradition of slavery with his historic Emancipation Proclamation, which read in part:

> [O]n the first day of January, A.D. 1863, all persons held as slaves within any State...the people whereof shall then be in rebellion against the United States shall be then, thenceforward, and forever free; and the executive government of the United States, including the military and naval authority thereof, will recognize and maintain the freedom of such persons and will do no act or acts to repress such persons, or any of them, in any efforts they may make for their freedom.

The famed proclamation freed only three-fourths of the more than four million African Americans held in bondage in the South. And the proclamation also granted "special slave-owning privileges" to those slave-owners in slave states not "in rebellion."

The historic Thirteenth, Fourteenth, and Fifteenth Amendments were gradually adopted after Lincoln's proclamation. Each amendment seemed to bring African Americans closer to becoming equal partners in the democratic experiment, to share in the rights promised by the United States Constitution.

The Thirteenth Amendment was adopted on December 18, 1865, and reads in part:

Neither slavery or involuntary servitude, except as punishment for a crime whereof the party shall have been duly convicted, shall exist within the United States or any other place subject to their jurisdiction.

The Fourteenth Amendment was adopted three years later, on July 28, 1868, and added further constitutional protections, declaring:

All persons born or naturalized in the United States, and subject to the jurisdiction thereof, are citizens of the United States and of the State wherein they reside. No State shall make or enforce any law which shall abridge the privileges or immunities of citizens of the United States; nor shall any State deprive any person of life, liberty, or property, without due process of law; nor deny to any person within its jurisdiction the equal protection of the laws.

Finally, on March 30, 1870, the Fifteenth Amendment "guaranteed" ex-slaves the right to vote:

The right of the citizens of the United States to vote shall not be denied or abridged by the United States or by any State on account of race, color, or previous condition of servitude.

In 1875, the Civil Rights Act added "full and equal enjoyment" of America's inns, transportation, etc., making discrimination against African Americans illegal.

The power of these impressive laws was short-lived. In 1896, a U. S. Supreme Court decision validated a so-called "separate but equal" doctrine that denied equality to millions of African Americans, in spite of legislation against racial discrimination.

Tried in 1896, the *Plessy v. Ferguson* case was an outgrowth of the "Jim Crow" laws that oppressed African Americans in the southern states. To counter the "equal protection" clauses of federal civil rights legislation, white southerners enacted state laws that regulated contact between the races in all public places, including rest rooms, restaurants, hotels, and public transportation. Separate facilities were designated for use by "Whites Only" and "Colored Only," with the facilities set aside for blacks being far inferior to those provided for whites. The era of "legal" racial segregation had begun.

These Jim Crow laws restricted African Americans to the dirty corners of bus stations, identified by signs that simply read "Colored." African Americans were also restricted to the back section of buses and were required by these laws to relinquish even that seating to white passengers when buses were over-crowded.

Homer Adolph Plessy, an African American, was arrested while traveling from New Orleans to Covington, Louisiana, for refusing to ride in the separate black railway car. By doing so he broke state law.

The case wound its way through the American justice system, finally reaching the U.S. Supreme Court. The High Court horrified African Americans and their supporters by ruling that the Fourteenth Amendment, which established and guaranteed citizenship regardless of race, "could not have been intended to abolish distinctions based on color or to enforce social...equality, or a commingling of the two races upon terms unsatisfactory to either."

Before the Civil War, Dred Scott attempted to secure his freedom through accepted legal means, by filing a lawsuit claiming he became free when his owner moved him into a free state. The U.S. Supreme Court denied his claim.

In dissenting, Supreme Court Justice Marshall Harlan wrote:

[I]n the eye of the law there is in this country no superior, dominant ruling class of citizens.... Our Constitution is color-blind and neither knows nor tolerates classes among citizens.... it is therefore to be regretted that this high tribunal...has reached the conclusion that it is competent for a State to regulate the enjoyment by citizens of their civil rights solely upon the basis of race. In my opinion, the judgment this day rendered will, in time, prove to be quite as pernicious as the decision made by this tribunal in the Dred Scott case. The thin disguise of equal accommodations for passengers in railroad coaches will not mislead anyone or atone for the wrong this day done.

The oppressive era of "Jim Crow" (taken from the name of a popular southern song) gripped the South with a "separate but equal" doctrine that was enforced by violence. From 1899 to 1917, more than three thousand blacks were lynched by their white fellow Americans.

Yet, even in the face of racial oppression, African Americans made great strides. In the early 1900s, Langston could look to heroic figures like Matthew Henson, a cabin boy turned

In the latter part of the nineteenth century, many states passed "Jim Crow" laws, segregating blacks from whites, requiring "separate but equal" schools, waiting rooms, rest rooms, and drinking fountains, all of which were clearly unequal in quality.

Arctic explorer, who accompanied Commodore Robert E. Peary on his historic trek to the North Pole.

And there was young Paul Leroy Robeson, son of an African-American minister, who won a scholarship to attend Rutgers University, one of the first of his race admitted to the prestigious school. Robeson would become not only the first African-American athlete at the school but also the first athlete of any race to be named to an All-American football team in the history of Rutgers.

There were many great men and women who paved the way and opened doors of opportunity for young African Americans like Langston Hughes, who became aware of these doors by reading the many books his grandmother and his teachers shared with him. Reading helped to pass the long lonely hours for an only child and it opened his mind to the wonders of African-American culture and the world at large.

Sadly, African Americans had few internationally famous professional sports figures except in the world of boxing, where Jack Johnson once ruled as heavyweight champion. And they were denied access to professional sports like baseball, America's most popular sport.

Some twenty or more African Americans

One of the great role models for young African Americans in the early 1900s was Matthew Henson, a member of Robert Peary's expedition to the North Pole. Henson had begun as a cabin boy but worked his way up to the status of full-fledged explorer.

had played in the major leagues by the mid-1880s, including Moses "Fleetwood" Walker, a barehanded catcher who played forty-one games for the Toledo Mudhens of the American Association in 1884. But in 1885, Adrian Constantine "Cap" Anson, white manager of the Chicago Cubs, forced through a resolution at a meeting of owners and managers to establish a "color line" that effectively barred African Americans from organized major league baseball until 1947.

Though there were few professional athletes who were role models for young African Americans, there were other great men and women they could look up to, many of them leaders in the struggle for full citizenship rights. None were more important than the NAACP's W.E.B. Du Bois, the editor of *The Crisis*.

From early in life Langston Hughes knew that there would be obstacles in his path. His grandmother and his *Crisis* readings kept him abreast of the problems faced by African Americans. He knew that he had to excel at his studies to become a "credit to the race," a member of W.E.B. Du Bois' "Talented Tenth," the "exceptional" African Americans who would be charged with saving the "Negro race," according to Du Bois.

Sadly, Grandma Mary died before Langston

finished grammar school, but she had given him a great deal, a strength of character that would benefit him for the rest of his life.

In his poem, "Mother to Son," Hughes must have had his grandmother in mind when he wrote:

Well, son, I'll tell you:
Life for me ain't been no crystal stair
It's had tacks in it,
And splinters.
But all the time
I'se been a-climbin' on,
And sometimes goin' in the dark,
So boy, don't you turn back....

Chapter Three

The Young Poet

WHEN HIS GRANDMOTHER died, young Langston was forced to move in with "Auntie" and "Uncle" Reed, family friends. They were kind and supportive, the wife a very religious woman, the husband much less religious but a hardworking and fair-dealing man. Langston liked them.

He read to pass the lonely days waiting for his mother to send for him. In books, Langston found a world filled with excitement and happy endings, where "if people suffered, they suffered in beautiful language.... And where most always the mortgage got paid off, the

When Langston Hughes decided to pursue a career as a writer, the most successful African-American poet was Paul Laurence Dunbar, acclaimed for his brilliant dialect poetry.

good knights won...." The real world, outside of the books that Langston learned to treasure, was awash with poverty and racism; and hope, at least for African Americans, was seldom fulfilled.

When Langston was not reading or in school, he took part-time work delivering newspapers and selling the popular *Saturday Evening Post* magazine. The pennies earned allowed him to attend an occasional movie, even though there were few movies that spoke to the entertainment needs of blacks.

In 1915, Hollywood released the now infamous D.W. Griffith film, *The Birth of a Nation.* African-American critics viewed the film as anti-Negro propaganda and were horrified when it became the first film to be shown at the White House.

African-American writer Lawrence Reddick pointed out that *The Birth of a Nation* "spoke to the emotions through the eyes. It showed for all to see that the South was *right* about the Negro, that the North was *right* about preserving the Union, that Reconstruction, which elevated Negroes and some poor whites, was a shameful thing, that the virtue of southern white womanhood had to be protected from Negro brutes, and that when all seemed lost, the Ku Klux Klan rushed in to save the day."

In 1915, Professor Carter G. Woodson

sought to present the true history of African Americans and founded the Association for the Study of Negro Life and History. Woodson, himself the son of former slaves, would devote his life to the cause of historical accuracy concerning blacks. He would become known as "the father of black history." Woodson was responsible for establishing the first celebration of Black History Week in 1926.

But poetry, most especially the poems of African-American writer Paul Laurence Dunbar, offered a more realistic and vibrant picture of African Americans. Langston saw a richness in Dunbar's "dialect" poetry that would later influence his own approach to poetry.

Born in Dayton, Ohio, in 1872, Dunbar was the son of a former slave. He rose from the relative obscurity of his birth to national acclaim by 1895 on the wings of his poetry. By the time of his death in 1906, Dunbar had written books of poetry, short stories, and several novels.

Writer and critic W.D. Howells praised Dunbar's work, writing: "These are the divinations and reports of what passes in the hearts and minds of a lowly people whose poetry had hitherto been inarticulately expressed in music, but now finds, for the first time in our tongue, literary interpretation of a very artistic completeness."

Though Dunbar enjoyed a great deal of success and fame from his dialect poetry, he was disheartened that it took attention away from his more serious work. (Something similar would happen to Langston Hughes at the height of his career.)

"You know, of course," said Dunbar, "I didn't start as a dialect poet. I simply came to the conclusion that I could write it as well [as], if not better than, anybody else I knew of, and that by doing so I should gain a hearing. I gained the hearing, and now they don't want me to write anything but dialect."

In his poem, "We Wear the Mask," Dunbar speaks of a double-consciousness that had been forced on African Americans:

We wear the mask that grins and lies,
It hides our cheeks and shades our eyes—
This debt we pay to human guile;
With torn and bleeding hearts we smile,
And mouth with myriad subtleties.

Dunbar's biographer, Benjamin Brawley, wrote that Dunbar's poetry "soared above race and touched the heart universal." In 1911, the *Encyclopedia Britannica* referred to Dunbar's poetry "as a distinct contribution to American literature, and entitles the author to be called

William Dean Howells was one of the most important white writers and critics at the end of the nineteenth century, and he offered strong praise and encouragement to Dunbar, opening the way for young African-American writers.

preeminently the poet of his race in America."

One of Dunbar's most popular poems, "When Malindy Sings," was one of Langston's favorites. It had rhythm, color, and excitement, connecting him directly to the unpretentious common folk.

G'way an' quit dat noise, Miss Lucy—
Put dat music book away;
What's de use to keep on tryin'?
Ef you practise twell you're gray,
You cain't sta't no notes a-flyin'
Lak de ones dat rants and rings
From de kitchen to de big woods
When Malindy sings.

Dialect poetry wasn't acceptable to all African Americans. Many critics denied that it had any artistic worth. Others charged that dialect poetry somehow celebrated the "worst" of the African-American race, without giving just attention to "successful and educated" blacks. Still, Hughes loved the art form and would later capture the folkish dialect of his people in a simple poem like "Bad Morning":

Here I sit
With my shoes mismated.
Lawdy-mercy!
I's frustrated!

By the early 1900s, there were a number of

African Americans expressing the heart and soul of black America through their poetry, short stories, and novels.

Langston Hughes became familiar with the works of Charles Waddell Chestnutt because the writer's daughter taught at the high school Langston attended. For over a decade, from 1879 to 1899, the fair-skinned Chestnutt wrote under assumed names. His writings, especially those such as "The Goophered Grapevine," were in the folk tradition and first appeared in *The Atlantic Monthly*. There is little doubt that Chestnutt's *Uncle Julius* stories, which were humorous and barbed looks at plantation life, had some influence on Hughes' future work.

By 1905, Chestnutt had written two books of short stories and three novels: *The House Behind the Cedars, The Marrow of Tradition,* and *The Colonel's Dream.* Though Chestnutt's shorter works generally explored the world of the common folk, his novels were poignant exposes of the world of the "tragic" mulatto, not black—not white!

W.E.B. Du Bois described Chestnutt as "of that group of white folk who because of a more or less remote Negro ancestor identified himself voluntarily with the darker group, studied them, expressed them, defended them, and yet never forgot the absurdity of this artificial position and always refused to admit its logic or its ethical sanction. He was not a Negro; he was a man...."

Chestnutt was a volatile spokesman against the absurdity of racism, writing that his purpose was "not so much the elevation of the colored people as the elevation of the whites—for I consider the unjust spirit of caste...a barrier to the moral progress of the American people...."

And Chestnutt warned, "The colored writer...has not yet passed the point of thinking of himself first as a Negro, burdened with the responsibility of defending and uplifting his race. Such a frame of mind, however praiseworthy from a moral standpoint, is bad for art."

A hungry reader, Langston was greatly moved by the works of Dunbar and white poet Carl Sandburg. But it wasn't until he was about to graduate from grammar school that Langston Hughes penned his first poem.

Hughes was fourteen years old when his mother, newly remarried, and employed, felt she was able to send for him. He thanked the Reeds for their kindness and moved to Lincoln, Illinois, where his mother lived. There he would finish grammar school and be elected class poet, though he had never, up to that point, written or even considered writing poet-

Hughes began to blossom as a poet while attending Central High School in Cleveland, Ohio, where he wrote for the school magazine, the Belfry Owl. Here he is seen with a group of his high school friends.

ry. In his autobiography, *The Big Sea,* Hughes suggests his appointment as class poet was due more to race than any real show of talent on his part. Hughes pointed out that his classmates, all white, knew that a poem had to have rhythm. And they believed, as did most whites, that "all Negroes can sing and dance, and have a sense of rhythm."

Still, Hughes took the position seriously. His first attempt at poetry was in celebration of class graduation. The poem, which he read aloud during graduation ceremonies, was in praise of the school's teaching staff. On that day, it seems, a poet was born.

Immediately after his graduation from grammar school, the family moved again. The family's next stop was Cleveland, Ohio, where Langston attended Central High School. It was there that he began to blossom as a poet and writer. He earned a post as a writer for the school magazine, the *Belfry Owl*. Young Langston turned his poetic eye to his close surroundings for subject matter. He would not write of flowers or beautiful weather. He found his inspiration in people—common folk who worked, struggled, and sometimes overcame, though they would seemingly be overwhelmed by their conditions.

And, as he created, he recalled his grandmother and the stories she told, writing in his autobiography, "Through my grandmother's stories always life moved, moved heroically toward an end. Nobody every cried...." There was laughter, rhythm, and warmth in Langston's early works. And there was depth and sensitivity, too.

Much later, an established writer, Hughes would explain that he always "felt the masses of our people had as much in their lives to put into books as did those more fortunate ones who had been born with some means."

Langston penned his first short story while a student at Central High School. The story, titled "Mary Winoski," was written as an assignment for his English class. It was well received by his instructor. All of his teachers recognized Langston's emerging talent and encouraged him whenever possible.

And it was while Hughes was still a high school student that he had his poetry accepted and published in *The Brownies' Book,* a literary magazine published just for young African Americans by the NAACP. The magazine, in a way, was the teen version of the civil rights organization's *The Crisis*.

It was through *The Crisis* magazine that Langston heard of Harlem. It seemed then a mysterious place that existed somewhere beyond his reach. Even so, he read of the excitement that was Harlem, the theaters, the great black actors and actresses; and he discovered great black writers who stirred his imagination.

In his autobiography, Hughes would confess that he "was in love with Harlem long before" he ever got there. The "dark side of Harlem intrigued" him. And he was fascinated by the fact that writers and entertainers like James Weldon Johnson, Jessie Fauset, Ethel Waters, Duke Ellington, Bert Williams, and Walter White lived there. Though Harlem was always on his mind, Langston Hughes would travel thousands of miles to even more exotic locales before ever reaching the so-called "Mecca" of black culture.

The 1910s were critical years in both American and African-American history. The acrid threat of world war had hung a dark cloud over the world since 1914, although the United States would not enter the conflict until three years later. On June 28, 1914, a Serbian national assassinated Austrian Archduke Franz Ferdinand and his wife in Sarajevo, triggering World War I. The United States would declare war on April 6, 1917.

Langston was barely in his teens at the onset of World War I. He watched as African-American men went off to war in the name of freedom, even though they did not enjoy complete freedom at home in America. Still, they

The CRISIS

APRIL 1923   15 cents the copy

The Crisis, *founded and edited by W.E.B. Du Bois as the voice of the NAACP, was the first major magazine to publish the works of Langston Hughes, including his best known poem,* "The Negro Speaks of Rivers."

went by the thousands. It was an irony that he would never understand. Over 300,000 African Americans served in the nation's armed forces during World War I.

African American servicemen returned, bloodied by a war to preserve freedom they had never experienced, and demanded equal rights. As editor of *The Crisis*, W.E.B. Du Bois trumpeted the cause of African-American GIs: "Today we return.... We return fighting. We return from fighting.... Make way for democracy! We saved it in France, and by Great Jehovah, we will save it in the United States of America."

Saving democracy in America would be a great deal more difficult than Du Bois imagined. While the war lasted years, the war against racism in America would last throughout the twentieth century.

And the war against racism would attract many voices. In 1914, Jamaican immigrant Marcus Garvey founded the United Negro Improvement Association, his aim to make "Africa be a bright star among the constellation of nations." His method was a back-to-Africa movement that caught the interests of thousands of African Americans who saw little hope for freedom in the United States.

By 1919 Garvey had established at least thirty branches of his United Negro

Improvement Association (UNIA) throughout the United States. Garvey's program was upbeat; a spectacle of flash and sass, with uniformed members parading proudly through the streets of Harlem.

Young Langston watched the excitement in Harlem from afar, dreaming one day of immersing himself in that font of black culture. While Langston dreamed of Harlem, he soon found that his father had plans for his future. Langston was six years old the last time he had seen his father. He was aware that James Hughes had prospered in Mexico, but he never gave much thought to living with him, that is, until his father's telegram arrived in early 1919.

Langston was surprised but somehow elated that his father wanted him to spend the summer with him in Mexico. He had not been to Mexico since the great earthquake that had changed his mother's plan of living there. Though his mother objected, Langston thought it important that he accept his father's invitation. It was especially important because the elder Hughes wanted to discuss plans for Langston's college education.

Chapter Four

The Red Summer

Langston Hughes was very uncomfortable when he learned that his father hated black people. It seemed ironic. But his father's hatred was far-reaching; he hated whites as well and was convinced that no black man would ever get a fair shake in the United States.

James Hughes was proud of his accomplishments in Toluca, Mexico. He was a successful rancher and a businessman. He felt—and was determined to convince his son—that such accomplishments would not have been possible for him in the United States, where

Langston occasionally visited his father, James Hughes, in Toluca, Mexico, where he had moved after becoming disillusioned with the United States because of its racial conflicts.

the color line was too oppressive.

The elder Hughes pointed to the great tide of black humanity rushing north to an imagined heaven from a very real hell in the South. Between 1916 and 1917, the black population increased forty-six percent in Chicago, Illinois, and fifty-five percent in Columbus, Ohio.

While the boll weevil and floods took their toll on the cotton crops in Louisiana, Mississippi, Alabama, Georgia, and Florida, the real reason for the great exodus of blacks from the South was the escalating racial violence. Thousands upon thousands of blacks rushed north, urged on by editorials in the *Chicago Defender.*

From the pages of the nation's black press came the call to black Americans in the South to leave! "Turn a deaf ear to everybody," advised Robert S. Abbott, publisher of the *Chicago Defender.* "You see they are not lifting their laws to help you.... Will they give you a square deal in court yet?... And our leaders will tell you the South is the best place for you. Turn a dead ear to the scoundrel, and let *him* stay."

Waves of blacks surged northward during the Great Migration in search of a "House of Refuge," an "Ark of Safety"—the "promised land." They would find much less. And the very blacks who had encouraged their migration would quickly turn a cold shoulder to them.

But "as the migration progressed," observed historian Allan H. Spears, "Negro leaders became increasingly aware of the problems presented by the newcomers.... Not only did the more established Negroes find the newcomers' habits personally offensive but they felt that they diminished the status of all Negroes in the eyes of the white community."

Even the militant *Defender* began to assail the immigrants with barbed editorials. "It is evident that some of the people coming to this city have seriously erred in their conduct in public places," chided the editors of the *Defender,* "much to the humiliation of all respectable classes of our citizens, and by so doing...have given our enemies ground for complaint."

There was no hope for African Americans North or South, concluded Langston's father. Why should a black man remain where he is not wanted, where he cannot make a decent living for his family, where he is indiscriminately brutalized and lynched?

Langston had no immediate answer. He knew that he loved black people, his people. And he knew that he could not cut himself off from them. He just could not find the words to explain his feelings to his father.

The elder Hughes pointed to the violence that was at that moment raging in the United States, violence directed against a segment of the American population due solely to the color of their skin.

During the period between July 13 and October 1, 1919, more than twenty-five race riots were recorded. The national death toll reached over one hundred. Eighty-three African Americans, many still in their country's uniform from the war, were lynched by white mobs during that terrible period that African-American writer James Weldon Johnson called "The Red Summer."

Federal troops were finally called in to restore order to Washington, D.C., Chicago, Illinois, Longview, Texas, and other cities, North and South.

In September of 1919, W.A. Domingo expressed the mood of African Americans in an article entitled "If We Must Die." The article appeared in *The Messenger,* a publication founded by A Philip Randolph and Chandler Owen in 1917. *The Messenger* was considered the "only radical Negro magazine" of the time. Domingo declared, on behalf of black Americans:

No longer are Negroes willing to be shot down or hunted from place to place like wild beasts;

Chandler Owen (above) joined with A. Philip Randolph in found-ing a new African-American magazine during World War I. The Messenger *was far more radical than* The Crisis, *calling on blacks to resist the growing white violence against them.*

no longer will they flee from their homes and
leave their property to the tender mercies of
the howling and cowardly mob. They have
changed, and now they intend to give men's
account of themselves. If death is to be their
portion, New Negroes are determined to make
their dying a costly investment for all concerned. If they must die they are determined
that they shall not travel through the valley
of the shadow of death alone, but that some
of their oppressors shall be their companions.

Though a pre-teen and teenager during this
chaotic period in American history, the young
Langston Hughes could not help but be aware
of the condition of African Americans in the
United States. The picture his father painted
was dark and foreboding. If he believed as his
father did, how could he ever opt to return to
the horror that awaited him as a black man
in the United States of America?

But he didn't believe as his father did. He
cringed at the brutality but somehow knew
that he could never run from it. He felt that,
through struggle, African Americans could
and would carve for themselves a meaningful
existence and role in developing America.
There was hope!

And Langston had faith, too, in the great
African-American men and women about
whom he read in the pages of *The Crisis*. How

could such great, intelligent, and determined men and women fail? There was indeed hope. Why couldn't his father see it too?

The summer in Mexico was not all negative, although Langston became sick and had to spend some time in the hospital. He also began to learn Spanish, a language that would become vital in his later work as a translator.

When summer was over, Langston returned to Cleveland to complete his final year of high school. He also had to begin to give serious thought to his future. He had already promised his father that he would return to Mexico the summer after graduation. Then his father would finalize his plans for Langston's college education. However, during the long train trip from Mexico to Cleveland, Langston realized that what he really wanted to be was a writer.

Langston's final year at Central High School was exciting. He was writing more and more. He had been elected class poet and appointed editor of the school yearbook. Still, his thoughts were on Harlem. Somehow he knew that he would find his destiny in the throbbing heart of that black community.

In 1920, as Langston Hughes prepared to graduate from Central High School and to choose his life's career, an ambitious and talented African-American man or woman could expect very little.

But from the East, from Harlem, came refreshing talk of a "New Negro." According to the editors of *The Messenger* (August 1920), the New Negro "demands political equality…, he demands the full product of his toil. His immediate aim is more wages, shorter hours, and better working conditions…, he stands for absolute and unequivocal *social equality*."

Alain Locke, scholar and social and literary critic, described the "Old Negro" as "more of a formula than a human being—something to be argued about, condemned, or defended, to be 'kept down,' or 'in his place,' or 'helped up,' to be worried with or worried over, harassed or patronized, a social bogey or a social burden."

W.E.B. Du Bois considered the future of African Americans to be in the able hands of a select group of "exceptional" black men and women. These he called the "Talented Tenth," a spearhead group that would clear the way for the masses of black people in America. "The problem of education," Du Bois believed, "among Negroes is the problem of developing the Best of this race that they may guide the Mass away from the contamination and death of the Worst, in their own and other races."

As part of his plan to develop a "talented tenth," Du Bois declared, in an article, "The Immediate Program of the American Negro"

Poet and editor Jessie Fauset was the earliest important writer to encourage Langston Hughes to seek a literary career. It was under her influence that his earliest writing saw publication.

(The Crisis, April 1915):

> In art and literature we should try to loose
> the tremendous emotional wealth of the
> Negro and the dramatic strength of his prob-
> lems through writing, the stage, pageantry,
> and the other forms of art. We should resur-
> rect forgotten ancient Negro art and history,
> and we should set the Black man before the
> world as both a creative artist and a strong
> subject for artistic treatment.

Hughes was convinced that his role was to
create, to "explain and illuminate the Negro
condition in America."

After graduation Langston reluctantly
boarded a train for Toluca, Mexico. He somehow knew that this trip would end more in
confrontation with his father than as a family reunion. He knew his father was steadfastly convinced that Langston should study mining engineering in Europe. It was not a plan
that appealed to the younger Hughes.

But Langston was also steadfastly convinced that education was the sword and
shield he would need to survive in a country
that denied him basic human rights. And, for
blacks, education was very difficult to acquire.

Excellence was the key ingredient to the
successes of African Americans like W.E.B. Du
Bois and Paul Robeson. There were a handful

of northern universities that tolerated the presence of African-American students if they were exceptional scholars. Even then there were no guarantees he would find a decent school to accept him.

A quick glance at the history of African Americans and higher education was disheartening. John Russwurm was considered one of the first African Americans to graduate from an American institution of higher learning. In 1826, Russwurm graduated from Bowdoin College in Maine. The following year, Russwurm and Reverend Samuel Cornish, a militant minister, founded the first African-American newspaper in the country, *Freedom's Journal.*

"We wish to plead our cause," Russwurm declared in his first editorial. "Too long have others spoken for us. Too long has the public been deceived by misrepresentations in things which concern us so dearly..., there are (those) who make it their business to enlarge upon the least trifle, which tends to... denounce our whole body for the misconduct of this guilty one.... Our vices and our degradation are ever arrayed against us, but our virtues are passed unnoticed."

Between 1826 and 1846, only twenty more African Americans would graduate from American colleges. It wasn't until after the

Civil War that institutions of higher learning for African Americans were constructed in any significant numbers. And it wasn't until a century after Russwurm's graduation, in 1826, that attending college became a priority among African Americans as more and more opportunities to gain a college education became available. By 1936, there were some forty thousand African-American college graduates in the United States.

James Hughes was determined to make Langston a businessman and mining engineer. Both were honorable and much needed professions. Both could provide a black man with an ideal life—*outside* the reach of the color line.

James Hughes put Langston to work as a bookkeeper on the ranch that he owned. Langston, his interests elsewhere, did a half-hearted job and failed miserably in his father's eyes. His father persisted in pushing Langston to excel at the work he gave him but quickly found that Langston resisted his persistence.

The day of confrontation came and Langston blurted out that he wanted to be a writer. Even more, he *was* a writer, recently published in two prestigious black magazines. Proudly, Langston showed his father his bylines in *The Brownies' Book* and in *The Crisis*.

The Brownie's Book had published several

The Brownies' Book

MARCH, 1920

BROWNIES LAND.

In addition to The Crisis, *the NAACP published a magazine for African-American children,* The Brownies' Book. *In it, in the early 1920s, editor Jessie Fauset printed several short stories and a children's play by Langston Hughes.*

short pieces, including a children's play, *The Gold Piece*. And, what would become one of Langston's best-known poems, "The Negro Speaks of Rivers," appeared in the pages of *The Crisis* in June 1921.

Langston seemed to write best when he was sad. "The Negro Speaks of Rivers" was written during the long train ride from Cleveland to Mexico. For Langston, the trip was one of the saddest periods in his life. The poem showed a feeling and depth that his earlier work had not. It was a powerful statement from the young poet, reading in part:

> I've known rivers:
> I've known rivers ancient as the world and
> older than the flow of human blood in
> human veins.
> My soul has grown deep like the rivers.

Langston showed his father the letter of support and encouragement from literary editor Jessie Fauset, an accomplished poet in her own right. He beamed that he was making major strides as a writer. "Yes," he boldly declared, "I want to be a writer!"

Langston felt the moment was his. He had declared himself a writer, which he hoped would shatter his father's dream of forcing him to study mining engineering. Langston's moment was overcome by his father's cold, calculating logic. When James Hughes demanded to know how much money he had earned from his writings, Langston could only reply, "None!" Sadly, few publications, even *The Crisis*, could afford to pay writers for their contributions.

James Hughes reminded his son that his mother was a college-educated woman, yet she was forced to wait tables in a restaurant to eke out a living. Was that what he wanted for himself? A series of jobs as busboy? Porter? Redcap? An underpaid servant to ill-mannered whites?

Though James Hughes had won the moment, Langston was not committed to his father's plans for him. He tried to cooperate over the next year in Mexico. But he spent all of his free time writing the poetry that would make him an internationally known and respected poet—though never a wealthy man!

Chapter Five

Harlem on My Mind

HARLEM WAS ON his mind, day in and day out. Langston Hughes could think only about Harlem, the Mecca of black culture. Even in Mexico, he felt he could hear the sounds of Harlem and see its magical sights as long as he could maintain his subscription to *The Crisis.*

Langston read everything he could about Harlem. In *The Autobiography of An Ex-Coloured Man,* author James Weldon Johnson provided Hughes with a vivid description of Harlem, writing:

Long before he ever went to New York, Langston Hughes was enchanted by what he had read and heard of the African-American community of Harlem and its blossoming culture.

If you ride northward the length of Manhattan Island, going through Central Park and coming out on Seventh Avenue or Lenox Avenue at One Hundred and Tenth Street, you cannot escape being struck by the sudden change in the character of the people you see. In the middle and lower parts of the city you have, perhaps, noted Negro faces here and there; but when you emerge from the Park, you see them everywhere, and as you go up either of these two great arteries leading out from the city to the north, you see more and more Negroes, walking in the streets, looking from the windows, trading in the shops, eating in the restaurants, going in and coming out of the theatres, until, nearing One Hundred and Thirty-fifth Street, ninety percent of the people you see, including the traffic officers, are Negroes. And it is not until you cross the Harlem River that the population whitens again, which it does as suddenly as it began to darken at One Hundred and Tenth Street. You have been having an outside glimpse of Harlem, the Negro Metropolis."

Harlem was not always the "Negro Metropolis." Initially a Dutch settlement and suburb of Manhattan, "Haarlem," as it was first spelled, experienced a sudden and expansive housing boom in the late 1890s and early

James Weldon Johnson's vivid description of Harlem in his autobiography intrigued Langston Hughes and reinforced his eagerness to move there as soon as possible after he had finished high school.

1900s. The "boom" was a major "bust" for white real-estate speculators who had counted on the development of mass transit in the area to fill their newly built apartments and houses.

The real-estate "bust," while disheartening for white landlords, became a "boom" for African Americans in need of room. The Great Migration of African Americans from the South had created a shortage of decent housing for blacks in an already tight and segregated market. Burdened by scores of unrented apartments and unsold houses, white building owners, against the very vocal resistance of white residents in Harlem, were forced to rent and sell to African Americans eager to move from the close quarters of the slum of Hell's Kitchen downtown.

Also, there was a concerted, often violent, effort on the part of whites in Hell's Kitchen to remove blacks from the area.

African-American realtors Philip A. Payton, J.C. Thomas, and John B. Nail recognized the opportunity for blacks to move into Harlem. They made contact with financially beleaguered landlords and were instrumental in securing properties for African Americans.

Change came slow and hard in Harlem. It wasn't until 1917 that the first African-American state assemblyman was elected to office. And, it wasn't until 1919 that a Harlem hospital hired its first African-American doctor and nurse. But African Americans thrived in the area, building churches and businesses and setting the stage for a period of literary and artistic awakening that would come to be known as the "Harlem Renaissance."

By 1920, in spite of obstacles, there were some eighty thousand African Americans living in Harlem, an increase of some thirty thousand since the beginning of the Great Migration during the war years. They brought with them their dreams of freedom, of prosperity, of proving themselves patriotic Americans. They also brought with them a rich culture, rooted in an African oral tradition that now expressed itself through song and theater. They brought with them their gospel music, their wailing mournful blues, and a rhythm that vibrated throughout Harlem.

Black music, wrote Du Bois in *The Crisis,* "has not only influenced American music, it has influenced American life; indeed, it has saturated American life. It has become the popular medium for our national expression musically. And who can say that it does not express the blare and jangle and the surge, too, of our national spirit?"

Even more, Du Bois saw black music, especially "the Negro folk song—the rhythmic cry of the slave—" as "the articulate message of the slave to the world..., the music of an unhappy people, of the children of disappointment; they tell of death and suffering and unvoiced longing toward a truer world... [They are] the singular heritage of the nation and the greatest gift of the Negro people."

It was in 1920 that the blues found its voice. Blues singer Mamie Smith recorded Perry Bradford's "Crazy Blues" on the Okeh label, and the era of "race records" (black music) began. This first blues recording was a surprising success. It sold 7,500 copies each week for months. Suddenly, the embryonic recording industry had discovered a new market. Soon, African-American entertainers like Jelly Roll Morton, Bessie Smith, Billie Holiday, Mahalia Jackson, Ella Fitzgerald, Duke Ellington, W.C. Handy, Muddy Waters, and countless others became household names in the homes of blacks *and* whites throughout the nation.

The blues growled from the raspy throats of hard-eyed men and tormented black women who exposed the tragic stories of millions of African Americans. And millions listened and danced to the swirling, thumping rhythms pumping from the heart and soul of black America. Few heard the cries for justice, free-

1925, by Edward Elcha, *courtesy of Rudi Blesh.*

The Harlem Renaissance was not just a literary movement. The African-American musical forms of blues and jazz flowered, with entertainers such as Bessie Smith leading the way.

dom, and equality that sponsored the words or the underlying determination and promise that a change was going to come.

The blues, observed African-American novelist Ralph Ellison *(Invisible Man),* "is an impulse to keep the painful details and episodes of a brutal experience alive in one's aching consciousness to finger its jagged grain, and to transcend it...."

Along with music came dance, "exotic jungle" contortions in the eyes of whites, lured into the hot, dark soul of Harlem by its surging, crashing rhythms—dance that was part of the attraction of all-Negro musicals, dance that rocked the dance floors of clubs throughout Harlem. The Lindy Hop and others were dances that whites struggled to learn on excursions into Harlem.

"Early in the Harlem literary renaissance period," wrote John Henrik Clarke *(Negro Digest,* December 1967), "the black ghetto became an attraction for a varied assortment of white celebrities and just plain thrill-seeking white people lost from their moorings. Some were insipid rebels, defying the mores of their upbringing by associating with Negroes on a socially equal level. Some were too rich to work, not educated enough to teach, and not holy enough to preach. Others were searching for the mythological 'noble savage'—

the 'exotic Negro.'"

And there was theater.

African Americans were treated poorly in early American theater, beginning with *The Padlock* (1769) by Isaac Bickerstaffe and Charles Dibdin. Billed as a "comic opera," it was little more than low comedy, featuring the one black cast member, Mungo, as a dialect spouting, profanity spitting, drunken West Indian slave.

The most insulting character to be introduced on the American stage was "Sambo," in the 1795 play, *The Triumph of Love* by John Murdock. The wide-eyed, grinning Sambo, somehow became symbolic of a time when "darkies" were happy as slaves. Stereotypes abounded on the American stage as minstrelsy, with white entertainers in blackface make-up, became popular. African Americans were variously and collectively seen as savage Africans, happy slaves, devoted servants, social delinquents, vicious criminals, and natural-born entertainers and musicians. It was in the blood!

The twentieth century in American theater ushered in a wave of negative stereotypes. The era of the black who was happy, bumbling, good-natured, afraid of the dark and ghosts, bugged of eye and wide of lip became part of the national character. These caricatures appeared in all manner of advertising and product packaging.

In the West, young African Americans like Oscar Micheaux used filmmaking as a tool to challenge stereotypes. As early as 1918, Micheaux was producing all-black silent films, though his productions never approached the technical quality of Hollywood productions, Micheaux's pioneering work in film ushered in the age of "race movies," produced by independent black-owned film companies.

The 1920s brought a new direction in African-American theater, vibrant and determined actors and producers such as Paul Robeson, Bert Williams, Flournoy Miller, Aubrey Lyles, Noble Sissle, and Eubie Blake.

Black writers began to write their own plays and stories, their pens becoming hammers to shatter the damning stereotypes that had haunted African Americans for decades.

"A people may become great through many means," charged writer James Weldon Johnson, "but there is only one measure by which its greatness is recognized and acknowledged. The final measure of the greatness of all peoples is the amount and standard of the literature and art they have produced.... No people that has produced great literature and art has ever been looked upon by the world as distinctly inferior."

In the theater during the Harlem Renaissance, performers such as Bert Williams led the way in breaking away from the old "Sambo" stereotypes that had been set by the minstrel shows of the nineteenth century.

Johnson had great confidence in black literature and culture, writing, "the Negro has already proved the possession of these [artistic] powers by being the creature of the only things artistic that have yet sprung from American soil and have been universally acknowledged as distinctive American products."

The task would not be easy, as pointed out by Doris E. Abramson, who observed, "[T]he Negro playwright's dilemma is that neither white nor black audiences can be counted on to support plays that attack or even question commonly accepted American mores."

Harlem was the base for all the excitement. Hughes knew it. "Negro arts flourished," recalled Hughes. "Books were written by and about Negroes. Jazz swept the nation, and the Savoy Ballroom on Lenox Avenue attracted all the great bands. New dances blossomed from the community streets—the Charleston, the Black Bottom, and the Lindy Hop....

"Harlem was heaven, then. Negro artists captured New York. Many had white patrons with money to spend and they spent it lavishly. The steps of Harlem town were light and gay. For many black and white Americans this was the millennium."

Langston very much wanted to be a part of the "millennium" in black culture.

"It was the next thing to Camelot," wrote Arna Bontemps, a Hughes contemporary, "to be young and a poet in the Harlem of those days."

A topical saying among African Americans of the time was, "I'd rather be a lamp post in Harlem than the governor of Georgia."

Of course, Langston wanted to be much more than a lamp post, a small swath of light on some dark corner. He wanted to immerse himself in the boiling cauldron that was the burgeoning Harlem Renaissance and renew himself.."

The only obstacle in Langston's path was his father. He wasn't certain that James Hughes would still agree to finance his college education if he didn't submit to an education in Europe. And, he knew he would have to learn to speak and write German proficiently if he was to excel at his studies as his father expected, even demanded.

During the year he spent in Mexico with his father, Langston searched for an answer, a compromise that possibly would satisfy, if not please, both him and his father. As it became time to make a decision, Langston proposed that he would, in fact, consider studies in mining engineering if he could attend Columbia University in New York.

James Hughes, of course, had little confidence in the education his son would receive attending an American institution. He was worried that racism would somehow interfere with or interrupt his son's studies. Europe, he was convinced, would be a better arena for young Langston to tackle his studies.

Langston persisted, finally convincing his father to allow him to go to Columbia. He still was not interested in the course of study outlined for him by his father, but his yearnings to see Harlem, to become a part of the cultural revolution, forced him to submit to his father's wishes.

In his autobiography, Hughes confesses that his only reason for accepting his father's offer and applying to Columbia was so that he could see Harlem.

When Langston Hughes graduated from high school, he visited his father in Mexico. James Hughes attempted to exert control over what Langson would do with his life by offering to pay for a college education but only if he would study for a career in mining engineering. At right, a view of Mexico City.

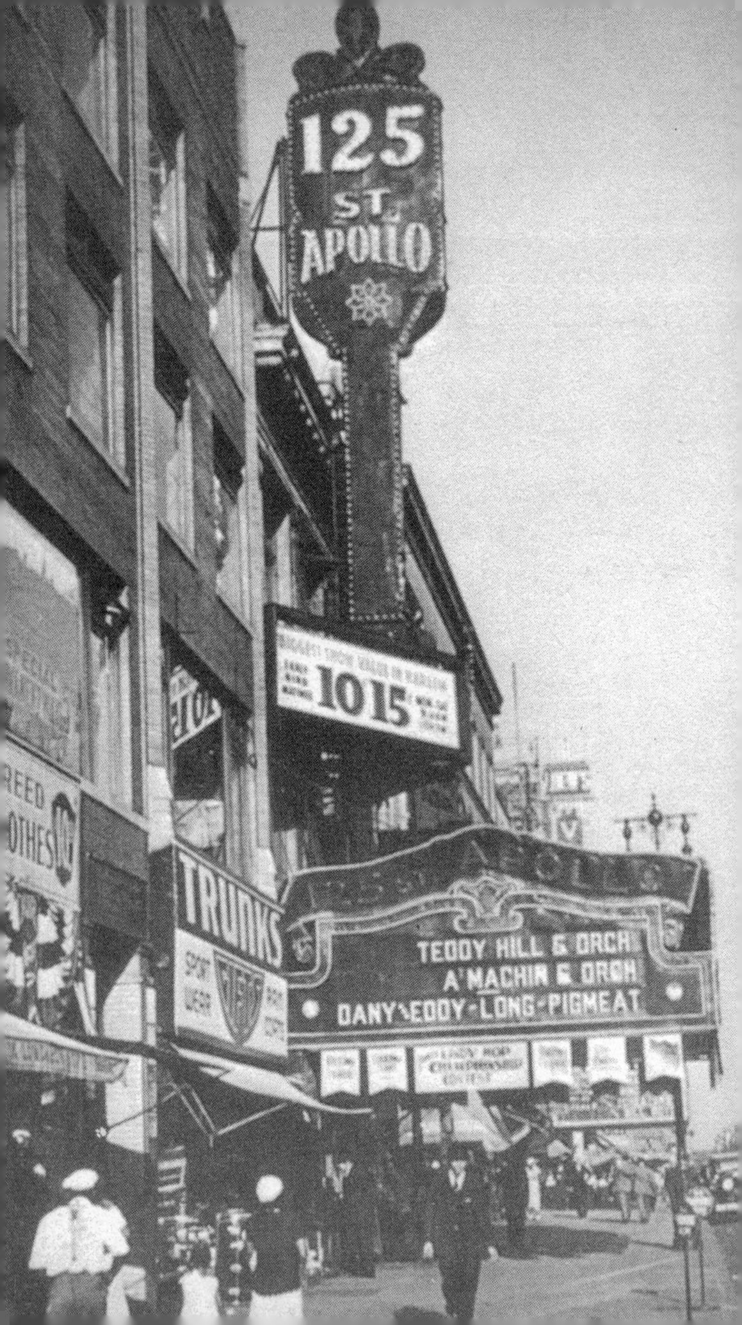
125
ST.
APOLLO
1015
TRUNKS
SPORT WEAR
TEDDY HILL & ORCH

Chapter Six

Harlem: the Mecca

LANGSTON HUGHES was nineteen when he climbed the stairway and exited the subway stop at Lenox Avenue and 135th Street. It was a warm September afternoon. Momentarily blinded by the sunlight, he slowly cleared his vision and, for the first time in his life, saw Harlem.

He was disappointed that none of the internationally known African-American entertainers like Duke Ellington were there to greet him. Still, he was elated. Harlem was more magical than he had ever imagined. It was hot, big, crowded, and best of all, it was *black*!

When Langston Hughes finally arrived in Harlem, he was like a kid in a candy store, excited by the theaters, the music, the libraries and bookstores, and by the creative people he met.

"I was in love with Harlem," Hughes would recall, "long before I got there."

Langston felt secure in Harlem. He checked into the Harlem branch of the Y.M.C.A., one of the few places where he could find a room in teeming Harlem. Once settled, he anxiously took a walking tour.

One of the first stops on Langston's impromptu tour was the Harlem Branch Library. From there he probably visited Young's Book Exchange, billed as "The Mecca of Literature pertaining to Colored People," located at 135 135th Street, between Lenox and Seventh avenues. The popular bookshop was founded by George Young in 1921, the first black-owned and black-oriented bookshop in Harlem. A one-time Pullman porter for the railroad, Young amassed an impressive collection of books by African-American authors. Among the many noted writers represented in his collection were W.E.B. Du Bois, J.A. Rogers, and Claude McKay.

Black Swan Records, the company that recorded Ethel Waters singing "Down Home Blues," had headquarters on Seventh Avenue near 135th Street.

Harlem was famous (infamous to some) for its many clubs and theaters. The blues and jazz bellowed from the interiors of nightspots like the Cotton Club. The theaters advertised hit all-black musicals like *Shuffle Along,* starring one of the most popular black performers of the day, Florence Mills.

Hughes took in a blues show at the Lincoln Theater, just across Lenox. He was trying to kill time until curtain time for *Shuffle Along* at the 63rd Street Theater. He knew that he could not—would not—sleep his first night in Harlem if he didn't see the hit musical and Florence Mills.

Mills was a hit in the show, which gained her roles in a number of other productions, including *Plantation Dover, Street to Dixie, From Dixie to Broadway,* and *Blackbirds.*

"*Shuffle Along* was a honey of a show," Hughes recalled. "Swift, bright, funny, rollicking, and gay, with a dozen danceable, singable tunes."

Responsibility forced Langston to put his love affair with Harlem on hold. He reluctantly checked out of the Harlem Y.M.C.A. and into Columbia University to begin his mining engineering studies.

He tried but just could not keep his mind on his courses. Harlem's allure was too strong. He daydreamed that if he were rich he "would have bought a house in Harlem and built musical steps up to the front door and installed chimes that at the press of a button played Duke Ellington tunes."

Although the patrons of the famed Cotton Club in Harlem were the rich white socialites from downtown New York, the popular nightspot was an important part of the Harlem Renaissance,

not only opening up the new black culture to the whites but also providing jobs and opportunities for young black entertainers to show their talent. Many great musicians got their start there.

They were not the thoughts a student of mining engineering should be harboring. And his dreams certainly did not mesh with his father's. It took little time for Langston to learn that he could no longer fulfill his father's wishes. By the end of his first year at Columbia, Langston had decided to give up his studies. He wrote his father to that effect, asking him not to send any more money, effectively ending his relationship with his father forever.

Harlem beckoned to Hughes, and he was drawn to it as a moth to a flame. He knew that he had found a home, one he would never leave. At least not for any great length of time.

Langston committed himself to his writing. He was fortunate enough to meet a few of the more important figures in the literary awakening, including Jessie Fauset. Though impressed with Langston's work, Fauset could do little to improve the young poet's financial situation. Few African-American writers made ends meet through their writing.

After a futile search for employment, Langston was forced to take a job on a truck farm on Staten Island. There, in exchange for food and board (in a hay barn), he toiled over acres of vegetables from dawn to long after dusk. It was hard work, but Langston somehow found enjoyment in working the land with

Marcus Garvey was an important part of the intellectual fervor of Harlem during the Renaissance, with his concept of a black-owned steamship line to transport blacks back to Africa.

the hardworking Greek farmers at his side.
Daily, the produce was trucked into Manhattan to be sold in the bustling produce markets.

A number of unrewarding jobs followed,
including a stint as a delivery boy for a florist.
The hours were long, the money meager, and
the boss overbearing. Langston quit and went
in search of other employment.

The streets of Harlem were alive with activ-
ity. From street-corner pulpits, self-appointed
preachers, philosophers and political activists—all angry orators—harangued crowds of
the unemployed, ragtag dark faces, refugees
"just up from the South," ex-GIs, brown and
black bodies who had donned olive drab for
democracy only to be Jim-Crowed at home,
and the frightened, the expectant, the curious,
and the confused.

The thunderous cry for freedom and justice
bellowed from the urban wilderness of brick
in uptown Manhattan. The collective roar
decried injustice. Racism! Demanded *equality!*
Change! Resistance! And there were the rum-
blings of *revolution!*

Marcus Garvey, a squat, fat, big-eyed West
Indian who had a penchant for military trap-
pings, parades, and fiery rhetoric and writings,
exhorted, "Back to Africa! To the Motherland!
Up you mighty race! Back to Africa! To the
Motherland!"

Countee Cullen was one of the many fine young African-American writers of the Harlem Renaissance. In his most famous poem, "Yet Do I Marvel," Cullen attacked racism.

It became not only a question of deciding who spoke for African Americans but also of finding a meaningful and positive definition of "African Americans." Who were they?

The cry from many corners was for a literature and art that worked as propaganda in challenging and overwhelming negative images of blacks in America.

Langston Hughes was not alone in his campaign to capture artistically and reveal the true nature of the African American. Other young poets and writers flocked to Harlem and quickly gained the attention of the older writers. Among the newcomers were Countee Cullen, a fiery young poet; Claude McKay, who had already stunned the world with his poem, "If We Must Die"; and, later, novelist/poet Arna Bontemps and the very talented and troubled Wallace Thurman, author of *The Blacker the Berry* and *Infants of Spring*.

All were eager, committed, energetic. "For such Negro artists as Langston Hughes, Countee Cullen, Jean Toomer, and Claude McKay," wrote Seymour L. Gross, "the depiction of life in the black ghetto was a serious attempt to grasp imaginatively their individual and group experiences, especially as these related to their sense of alienation and their glowingly reconstructed (if somewhat fantasized) 'African inheritance.'"

Claude McKay published several collections of poetry during the Harlem Renaissance, but his "If We Must Die" may have been the single greatest poem of the time, though it outraged many whites, including Senator Henry Cabot Lodge.

All of these young writers ignored the lives of the middle- and upper-class African Americans and focused their artistic eyes on the common folk. Oddly, as Hughes later pointed out, "The ordinary Negroes hadn't heard of the Negro Renaissance. And if they had, it hadn't raised their wages any."

Still the young writers charged ahead, young bulls willing to take on all comers.

Countee Cullen, reared in a Methodist parsonage, was born in 1903 in New York. Like Langston Hughes, he won poetry contests while still in high school. He was praised as a "Harlem prodigy" and quickly became a major contributor to the literature of the renaissance period.

Cullen's most famous poem, "Yet Do I Marvel," was a direct assault on racism:

I doubt not God is good, well-meaning, kind,
Yet do I marvel at this curious thing:
To make a poet black, and bid him sing!

Later in their careers, Hughes and Cullen offered a special edition of their poetry at special rates. They wanted to make their work affordable to the African-American community, as the majority of the books published at the time were in hardcover and somewhat expensive.

In 1922, Claude McKay, one of the stellar poets of the day, published a collection of poems, *Harlem Shadows.* His first book of poetry, *Songs of Jamaica,* was published when he was just nineteen years old. The young poet, who had been born in Jamaica, attended Tuskegee Institute and Kansas State University as an agriculture student, but his strength was his powerful and sensitive poetry. His poem "If We Must Die" was so disturbing to some whites that it prompted Senator Henry Cabot Lodge to read the fiery piece into the Congressional Record as proof of escalating black militancy.

The action did not silence McKay's acid poetry. He titled a poem "America" and wrote:

Although she feeds me bread of bitterness,
And sinks into my throat her tiger's tooth,
Stealing my breath of life, I will confess
I love this cultured hell that tests my youth.

And, in his poem "The White House" (which did not refer to the president's home), he declared:

Your door is shut against my tightened face,
And I am sharp as steel with discontent;
But I possess the courage and the grace
To bear my anger proudly and unbent.

There were a number of publications eager to print the works of the young writers, though little money changed hands. The most popular weekly of the time, the *Chicago Defender,* had increased its circulation from 10,000 subscribers in 1916 to 283,571 by the beginning of the 1920s. African Americans were becoming avid readers.

Hughes was immediately caught up in the historic time. He wrote whenever he could, generally late at night and early in the morning. But his priority was finding work, almost any kind of work, as his thinning bankroll led to desperation. As winter approached, Langston took a job aboard a derelict ship, one of hundreds rusting in a New York harbor. His job was to see that none of the unseaworthy ships broke free of their moorings.

Langston seldom left the ship. And as winter settled over the rusting hulks, he settled in to read and write. By spring he had amassed a great deal of material. But his financial situation was no better. Almost as a last resort, he took a job as mess boy aboard the *SS Malone,* a tramp steamer sailing for the Azores and Africa.

It was a solemn moment as the rusting steamer crept out of the New York harbor. Langston took a last, longing look at the city of his dreams and then, in a private ritual, threw his collection of books into the sea.

In his autobiography, Hughes explains the seemingly bizarre action as symbolic, "like throwing a million bricks out of my heart—for it wasn't only the books that I wanted to throw away, but everything unpleasant and miserable out of my past: ...I wanted to be a man on my own, control my own life, and go my own way. I was twenty-one."

Chapter Seven

World Traveler

LANGSTON HUGHES was a seasoned world traveler by the time he once again settled in Harlem. They both had changed: Hughes had become more worldly and wiser; Harlem had grown into a roiling sea of black faces surging along the wide avenues. Still, it was home, and, in that respect, nothing had changed.

While a mess boy aboard the *SS Malone*, Hughes had sailed to scores of ports of call along the coast of West Africa, the Ivory Coast, the Gold Coast, and the Congo. It was a mag-

Before he returned to Harlem, Langston Hughes traveled throughout Europe and visited many parts of Africa, especially the countries along the West Coast, such as Liberia.

ical, firsthand tour of the Motherland, a tour of discovery. He learned that, in many places in Africa, he, a black man, was considered more white than black. It was an irony that gave Hughes pause to think and reevaluate his role as an African American. More and more he came to realize that his home was Harlem, U.S.A. It was the only place in the world where he was truly free to be himself.

Hughes didn't immediately resettle in Harlem after his working tour of Africa, the Canaries, and the Azores. He visited his mother in McKeesport, leaving Jocko, his pet monkey, as an unwanted guest, before being lured back to the sea and further adventure.

Hughes would next take a job aboard a freighter sailing for Holland. He enjoyed the trip to Rotterdam and the company of his shipmates so much that he stayed aboard the ship for a second run from New York to Rotterdam. This time, however, Langston did not return to America on the freighter. A number of accidents and mishaps aboard the ship convinced Hughes that the ship might be jinxed. He drew down his pay, about twenty-five dollars, and took a train to Paris, the City of Lights.

Visiting Paris was a dream come true for Langston, on a par with his dream of seeing Harlem. But the dream quickly turned nightmarish when his funds ran out and he was forced to seek employment. Well-paying jobs were no easier to secure in Paris than in the United States. It was a bleak, hungry, and cold period for Langston, until he finally got a job as second cook at the Grand Duc nightclub in Paris. The title was misleading, for he worked as the dishwasher.

The meager income allowed Langston to eat, find lodging, and also take in some of the magical sights of Paris. Whenever he could, he traveled, exploring the European continent from Paris to Genoa.

In Italy, his money stolen, Hughes resorted to beachcombing to survive. He worked at odd jobs in Genoa until he was able to secure a "workaway" position on a freighter sailing for New York. He was finally heading home to Harlem.

Upon his return to the United States, Hughes could boast, "I live in the heart of Harlem. I have also lived in the heart of Paris...and Mexico City. The people of Harlem seem not very different from others, except in language. I love the color of their language and, being a Harlemite myself, their problems and interests are my problems and interests."

In his autobiography, Hughes recalls that he had sailed from the United States with eight dollars to return with a quarter. He had seen Europe for $7.75!

Wearied by and wiser from his world travels, Hughes visited his mother in Washington, D.C., before immersing himself in the problems and interests of Harlem. And there was still the problem of employment, or the lack thereof, that was a major concern for him.

There were few jobs open to African Americans, even in the nation's capital. And, armed only with a high-school diploma, Hughes could not hope to compete with better educated African Americans who were struggling as he was for employment.

Just as Hughes was about to give up his search for work, a family member intervened and helped him land a job with Carter G. Woodson. Langston's job was as a researcher for Woodson's *Journal of Negro History*. However, the free-spirited poet soon became bored with his monotonous duties and quit.

Money was still a priority in Langston's life, so he took a job as a busboy at the Wardman Park Hotel in the city. He was writing more and more, mainly because he was not happy in Washington. And, while published and the subject of some praise for his work, Hughes had yet to gain national attention, especially the attention of influential whites. He was also not making any money from writing.

By 1925, the poems of Langston Hughes had appeared in a number of prestigious publica-

Upon returning to the United States, Hughes moved to Washington, D.C., to be near his mother. Although the Great Depression was still a few years off, jobs for African Americans in the nation's capital were already scarce.

tions, including *The Crisis, Current Opinion, Southern Workman, Les Continents, Opportunity,* and *Survey Graphic.*

While still on his "Parisian holiday," Hughes had met Dr. Alain Locke, who at the time was editing a special issue of *Survey Graphic.* Dr. Locke had been invited by *Survey Graphic* founder-editor Paul Underwood Kellogg to guest-edit an issue that would focus on Harlem, "The Greatest Negro Community in the World."

Dr. Locke explained that he was impressed by Hughes' earlier work, which he had read in *The Crisis,* especially his poem, "The Negro Speaks of Rivers." Hughes was surprised to find that the well-respected scholar wanted him to contribute some of his work to the landmark issue of *Survey Graphic.*

The work of Dr. Locke culminated with the publication of Volume VI, No. 6, of the *Survey Graphic* in March of 1925. The issue sold out its initial print run of thirty thousand copies in less than two weeks. Twelve days after the release of the March issue, another twelve thousand copies were printed to satisfy a hungry reading public.

The Locke-edited issue was divided into three sections:

I. The Greatest Negro Community in the World

II. The Negro Expresses Himself
III. Black and White—Studies in Race
    Contacts

In the introduction to the special issue of
Survey Graphic, entitled, "Harlem: Mecca of
the New Negro," Dr. Locke provided a defini-
tive description of the subject of the work:

Here in Manhattan is not merely the largest
Negro community in the world, but the first
concentration in history of so many diverse
elements of Negro life. It has attracted the
African, the West Indian, the Negro
American; has brought together the Negro of
the North and the Negro of the South; the
man from the city and the man from the town
and village; the peasant, the student, the
business man, the professional man, artist,
poet, musician, adventurer and worker,
preacher and criminal, exploiter and social
outcast. Each group has come with its own
separate motives and for its own special ends,
but their greatest experience has been the
finding of one another.

His fortunes quickly changed. In 1925,
Langston's poem, "The Weary Blues" won first
prize in a contest held by *Opportunity* magazine. The poem, one he had worked on for some
time, read in part:

I got de weary blues
And I can't be satisfied.
Got de weary blues
And can't be satisfied.

The poem tapped into the raw soul of black
America, a soul frustrated by the color line,
wearied by racial oppression. Hughes called it
his "lucky poem."

At a dinner party held in celebration of the
contest winners, noted author (and lyricist for
"Lift Every Voice and Sing," the Black
National Anthem) James Weldon Johnson
read Hughes' winning poem to the guests.
Zora Neale Hurston and poet Countee Cullen
were also award winners that night.

It was a memorable night for Langston
Hughes. The most powerful and most brilliant
African Americans were present to celebrate
his talent. Prominent whites were also in
attendance. And that evening the young poet
was introduced to Carl Van Vechten, who liked
his work.

Van Vechten, an editor at Alfred A. Knopf,
was a successful novelist, with three books to
his credit: *Peter Whiffle, The Blind Bow-Boy,*
and *The Tattooed Countess.* He had a reputation for encouraging young black writers and
persuading major publications like *Vanity Fair*
to print their works.

The period when Hughes lived in Washington represented a turning point in his career. Not only was he recognized with an Opportunity magazine award, but it was while he was working as a waiter that poet Vachel Lindsay "discovered" him.

Hughes was elated by Van Vechten's interest and praise. Although he knew that his accomplishments would not impress his father, Langston was proud. And he was speechless when he found that Van Vechten wanted to submit a collection of his work to publisher Alfred A. Knopf. Hughes had been writing furiously since his return to the United States. He had a treasure chest of poems ready to submit.

Immediately after the gala event, Langston rushed home to Washington. He gathered his best poems, including "The Weary Blues" and "The Negro Speaks of Rivers," and mailed them to Van Vechten. Then there was nothing left to do but wait and work!

The job at the Wardman Park Hotel was dreary and routine for Langston. Then one day Langston learned that Vachel Lindsay, one of the most respected poets of the day, had taken rooms in the hotel. Langston had read Lindsay's poetry and desperately wanted to share his own work with the renowned poet. When Lindsay dined at the hotel's restaurant, Hughes daringly slipped some of his poems onto Lindsay's table without a word and walked away.

Hughes spent a nervous night, wondering what Lindsay's reaction to his poetry would be. Had he simply thrown it into the trash

Editor and scholar Alain Locke was one of the many influential literary figures who encouraged Langston Hughes and published his work. He was also a good friend to the young writer.

when he discovered it? Had he read it, then tossed it aside as amateurish rhymes? Or maybe he had given Lindsay the wrong poems to read; he had left three—"Jazzonia," "The Weary Blues," and "Negro Dancers." Were they good enough?! Wasn't "The Weary Blues" his "lucky poem?"

The next day Langston was stunned to find that Lindsay had read his poems, liked them, and then shared his "discovery" with the press. The day's paper featured a major story about Lindsay's discovery of a "busboy poet." The story quickly gained national attention, giving Langston the first publicity break of his young career.

Lindsay presented Hughes with books of poetry and urged in a personal note, "Do not let any lionizers stampede you. Hide and write and study and think. I know what factions do. Beware of them. I know what flatterers do. Beware of them. I know what lionizers do. Beware of them." The note was dated December 6, 1925.

Celebrity status was more than Langston could readily handle. He became the object of considerable attention. People flocked to the hotel to "see" the busboy poet. The attention was so overwhelming that Langston was forced to quit his job in order to maintain peace of mind. After a tiring search, he final-

Carl Van Vechten, an editor at the Alfred A. Knopf publishing house, helped Hughes get his poems printed in major magazines such as Vanity Fair. *Eventually Van Vechten would publish Hughes' first volume of poetry,* The Weary Blues.

ly found work at a fish and oyster restaurant in Washington.

The chance meetings with Vachel Lindsay and Carl Van Vechten earned more than superficial celebrity status for the young poet. He soon found that mainstream magazines like *Vanity Fair,* the *New Republic,* and *Bookman* were interested in printing not only his work but also the works of other young poets, like Hughes' protege Countee Cullen. More importantly, these publications paid money to the writers!

The fees, some larger than others, were received gratefully by the financially strapped Hughes. He began to feel that he really was a writer, and he began to take his work more seriously.

After his poetry won a contest sponsored by *The Crisis* magazine, Hughes knew that he was now actively involved in the great literary awakening of the Harlem Renaissance. He felt he was one of Du Bois' "talented tenth," prepared, pen in hand, to defend the race and, as Du Bois mandated, to "guide the Mass away from the contamination and death of the Worst...."

Hughes was lacking only in that he did not have a college education, like so many of the other young writers who now made Harlem their home and the subject of some of their work. He knew that he could never hope to fulfill his mission if he did not himself excel, which meant that he needed to complete his aborted college studies.

Of course, money was still a major stumbling block for Langston. He knew that he could not depend on his low-paying jobs as a source of college tuition. His mother's financial situation was little better than his own, and he would not turn to his father for assistance.

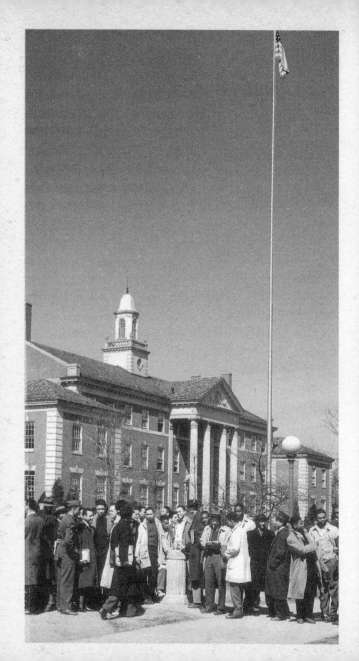

Chapter Eight

College Bound

HUGHES WAS ANXIOUS to attend college, but he was aware that he could not depend solely on his writing to survive. He could never hope to make a living from the sporadic checks from the few magazines willing to publish his work.

He was now having misgivings about having given up his studies at Columbia University, for he had begun to recognize the importance of a college education for an African American in twentieth-century America. He now saw that it was imperative that he earn a diploma.

It was only after he began to achieve some success as a poet that Hughes regretted having dropped out of college. Because he was living in Washington, he considered enrolling at Howard University, one of the most important black colleges.

He made inquiries at a number of colleges, including Howard University. Located in the nation's capital, Howard, like scores of other historically black institutions of higher learning, was founded shortly after the end of the Civil War. Howard was created in 1867 and named for Oliver Otis Howard, a white Union general during the Civil War and the commissioner of the Freedmen's Bureau after the war.

The Freedmen's Bureau was created by an act of Congress in 1865, remaining in existence until 1872. As commissioner of the bureau, Howard was responsible for aiding in the transition from slavery to freedom of some four million ex-slaves and refugees of the devastating Civil War.

The problems faced by Howard and the bureau were numerous, the most basic being providing food, medicine, clothing, and other necessities to the newly freed slaves. The bureau also undertook to protect the freed slaves from anti-Negro violence and efforts to keep them in slavery in the South.

One of the most important functions of the Freedmen's Bureau was the founding of schools like Howard University, as a part of the attempt to combat the high illiteracy rate among slaves who, by law, had been denied education before the war.

Howard was founded on the site of a farm in the District of Columbia. Over its long history, it would proudly claim as graduates a quarter of African-American lawyers and almost half of the African-American doctors, engineers, dentists, and architects in the country.

Howard seemed the ideal choice for Hughes to pursue his higher education; not only was it one of the most prestigious of black colleges but it was also in Washington, D.C., where he was living and working at the time. But then one day while in New York, he met a wealthy white patron of the arts who was interested in his work. During the course of the friendly conversation, Hughes mentioned his dream of returning to college. The patron offered to help him to enroll at Lincoln University in Chester County, Pennsylvania.

It was a miracle as far as Hughes was concerned. He had already met another young poet who was a student at Lincoln, and the student had told him that Lincoln was the perfect place for a writer.

Hughes quickly accepted the patron's offer. There was nothing to consider. He enrolled at Lincoln that winter and began his college education in earnest.

Lincoln University was one of the oldest historically black colleges in the nation, having

It was through the influence of a wealthy white patron that Hughes was persuaded to enroll at Lincoln University in Chester County, Pennsylvania, in order to complete his education.

Lincoln was one of the oldest "historically black" colleges in the United States, having been founded in 1854 by a Presbyterian minister. Hughes found the school intellectually stimulating.

been founded at Oxford, Pennsylvania, in 1854 by Reverend John Miller Dickey and his wife. Reverend Dickey was a Presbyterian minister and the son of a minister. He took his ministry seriously, and he had braved violence to serve as a missionary in the South to preach to slaves in Georgia.

When Lincoln opened its doors for "the scientific, classical, and theological education of colored youth of the male sex," slavery was still the law of the land in the South. (Today Lincoln University is co-educational.)

Hughes found himself in impressive company at Lincoln. Thurgood Marshall (who would become a U.S. Supreme Court Justice) and Cab Calloway (who would become a noted bandleader) were also students there at the time.

Langston was pleased with his course of study, but he could not help noticing something very odd about the racial makeup of the faculty. Though Lincoln had an all-black student body, it was operated and maintained by an all-white administrative staff and faculty.

Hughes was puzzled by the lack of African Americans on the staff of a school that professed to educate and train "Negro leaders." Weren't they aware that W.E.B. Du Bois had already defined the role of the historically black college? It was a role that Lincoln could not hope to fulfill with an all-white faculty.

After his first volume of poetry, The Weary Blues, *was published in 1926, Hughes visited the famed Tuskegee Institute with Jessie Fauset (left) and Zora Neale Hurston (right).*

"The function of the Negro College then," wrote Du Bois, "is clear: it must maintain the standards of popular education, it must seek the social regeneration of the Negro, and it must help in the solution of problems of race contact and cooperation."

Hughes challenged the racial composition of the Lincoln faculty as part of a sociology project for a Professor Larabee. He meticulously surveyed the upperclassmen, juniors and seniors, and asked them candidly whether or not they objected to the all-white faculty. Didn't it somehow contend, or at least infer, that African Americans were incapable of educating and training their own leaders?

Hughes encouraged Thurgood Marshall to join him in his crusade to integrate the faculty, but he was reluctant, as were most of the rest of his fellow students.

The survey triggered an unexpected controversy. Hughes was shocked to discover that sixty-three percent of the upperclassmen preferred an all-white faculty. Many told him candidly that they did not feel that black instructors were qualified to train them for leadership.

How could African Americans criticize their own? Hughes asked, but could find no ready answer. He was beginning to see that blacks were too often pawns, moved whimsically by white hands in a game where the rules were fashioned along color lines. Had his father been right? Was there no hope for an African American in the United States? No place where he might freely express his "dark-skinned self?"

In the *Nation* magazine, Hughes expressed his deepest feelings in a scathing article that became known as his "manifesto."

The Negro artist works against an undertow of sharp criticism and misunderstanding from his own group and intentional bribes from the whites. "Oh, be respectable, write about nice people, show how good we are," say Negroes. "Be stereotyped, don't go too far, don't shatter our illusions about you, don't amuse us too seriously. We will pay you," say the whites.... We younger Negro artists who create now intend to express our individual dark-skinned selves without fear or shame. If white people are pleased we are glad. If they are not, it doesn't matter. We know we are beautiful. And ugly too. The tom-tom cries and the tom-tom laughs. If colored people are pleased we are glad. If they are not, their displeasure doesn't matter either. We build our temples for tomorrow, strong as we know how, and we stand on top of the mountain, free within ourselves.

The shallowness not only of his fellow students but also of supposedly sophisticated and proud African-American professionals hurt Hughes deeply. He saw them as denying their cultural identity, their racial worth. He would later write, "[T]his is the mountain standing in the way of any true Negro art in America—this urge within the race toward whiteness, the desire to pour racial individuality into the mold of American standardization, and to be as little Negro and as much *American* as possible."

In 1926, Knopf published *The Weary Blues,* the first collection of poetry by Langston Hughes. Van Vechten wrote a laudatory introduction for the book, celebrating the young poet's talent and future as a writer. In the parlance of the time, Langston Hughes was a "credit to the race."

The Weary Blues was an immediate success. The work contained sixty-eight poems, including his most famous one, "The Negro Speaks of Rivers," and his "lucky poem," after which the book was titled. The book quickly sold twelve hundred copies, a successful print run, given the times and the subject matter.

The interest in Langston's poetry was high in 1926. Among the many magazines printing his work was the *Saturday Review,* which published the poem "Mulatto."

One of Hughes' classmates at Lincoln was Thurgood Marshall, who would later lead the battle for civil rights in the law courts. However, during his student days, Marshall refused to join Hughes' protest against the all-white nature of the school faculty.

But late in 1927, Hughes and his young peers in the Harlem Renaissance embarked on a project that failed miserably.

Fire!! was the name chosen for the publication founded by Hughes (still a student at Lincoln) and Harlem-based writers and artists Wallace Thurman, Zora Neale Hurston, Aaron Douglas, John P. Davis, Bruce Nugent, and Gwendolyn Bennett. The stated goal of the newly founded publication was to "burn up a lot of the old, dead conventional Negro-white ideas of the past."

The young writers were committed, but their sincere efforts aside, they seemed doomed to failure. The entrenched African-American leadership and the majority of the members of the African-American press were not amused or impressed by the first issue of *Fire!!*

Rean Graves of the *Baltimore Afro-American* was vehemently opposed to the continued publication of *Fire!!* He criticized it as an insult to African Americans and angrily wrote: "I have just tossed the first issue of *Fire* into the fire.... Aaron Douglas, who, in spite of himself and the meaningless grotesqueness of his creations, has gained a reputation as an artist, is permitted to spoil three perfectly good pages and a cover with his pen and ink hodgepodge. Countee Cullen has written a beautiful poem in his 'From a Dark Tower,' but tries his best to obscure the thought in his superfluous sentences. Langston Hughes displays his usual ability to say nothing in many words."

Sadly, the magazine even drew the wrath of W.E.B. Du Bois. And the unsold issues of *Fire!!*, Volume 1, Number 1, stored in a basement for safekeeping, ironically were destroyed in an accidental fire.

The black elite hungered for art that would celebrate their accomplishments, that would present the white world with a positive, uplifting portrait of their race. Hughes and his peers sought to capture the soul of the African American alive, they felt, only in ordinary people. The black elite wanted self-serving propaganda. Hughes and writers like Wallace Thurman had other plans for their work.

"All art no doubt is propaganda," Wallace Thurman declared on behalf of young black artists, "but all propaganda is most certainly not art."

In 1927, publisher Alfred A. Knopf, influenced by Carl Van Vechten, published a second volume of poetry by Langston Hughes. The collection appeared under the misleading and misunderstood title, *Fine Clothes to the Jew.* The title referred to blacks pawning their "fine clothes" when times were hard. Because many of the pawnshops in Harlem were owned by Jews, Harlemites coined the phrase "fine clothes to the Jew," which became a popular expression on the streets of the community.

Once again, Hughes found himself on the wrong end of barbed criticism. Oddly, the black press led the assault against the poet and, more particularly, his latest collection of poems, *Fine Clothes to the Jew*. The literary critic for the Chicago *Whip* rapped Hughes as "the poet lowrate of Harlem."

The *Pittsburgh Courier* and the *Afro-American* attacked Hughes' poetry for being "vulgar, illiterate, non-artistic pieces of trash."

The press claimed that Hughes and writers of his kind did little to advance the cause of African Americans and more to further negative stereotypes. They charged that whites like Carl Van Vechten exerted too much influence over the works of black writers like Hughes.

In an article that appeared in *The Crisis* magazine, Hughes defended himself against the assaults from the black press and especially the alleged influence Van Vechten had on his writings. "I would like herewith to state and declare," Hughes wrote, "that many of the poems in said book [*Fine Clothes to the Jew*] were written before I made the acquaintance of Mr. Van Vechten.... Those poems which were written after my acquaintance with Mr.

Van Vechten were certainly not about him, not requested by him, some of them not liked by him, nor, so far as I know, do they in any way bear his poetic influence."

Though Hughes was not influenced by Van Vechten, by white editors, or by patrons, he did recognize the irony of his position as an African-American poet involved in a so-called "black literary awakening."

Writer/historian Margaret Walker explains that "Rich white patrons or 'angels' who could and did underwrite the poetry of Negroes by helping to support Negroes who were interested in writing poetry did so as a fad to amuse themselves and their guests at some of the fabulous parties of the Twenties. They considered the intelligent, sensitive, and creative Negro as the talented tenth, an exotic, bizarre, and unusual member of his race; and they indulgently regarded the poetry of the Negro as the prattle of a gifted child."

Sadly, Hughes had also learned "that it was seemingly impossible for black Harlem to live without white downtown. My youthful illusion that Harlem was a world unto itself did not last very long. It was not an area that ran itself. The famous nightclubs were owned by whites, as were the theaters. Almost all the stores were owned by whites, and many at that time did not even (in the very middle of

Harlem) employ Negro clerks. The books of
Harlem writers all had to be published downtown, if they were to be published at all.
Downtown: *white*. Uptown: *black*. White downtown pulling all the strings in Harlem.... And
almost all of the policemen in Harlem were
white. Black Harlem really was in white face,
economically speaking."

Hughes was prompted to write the following poem as an expression of his rebellion
against the interference of whites or blacks,
where his work was concerned.

Because my mouth
Is wide with laughter
And my throat
Is deep with song,
You do not think
I suffer after
I have held my pain
So long?

Because my mouth
Is wide with laughter,
You do not hear
My inner cry?
Because my feet
Are gay and dancing,
You do not know
I die?

There was now little doubt in Hughes' mind that the African-American artist was considered more freak than prodigy. "Here are our problems," he observed in an angry article. "Negro books are considered by editors and publishers as exotic. Negro materials are placed, like Chinese materials or Bali materials, into certain classifications. Magazine editors tell you, 'We can use but so many Negro stories a year.'... When we cease to be exotic, we do not sell well."

It was a problem that would dog his steps throughout his career as a writer.

Chapter Nine

Harlem in Vogue

LIFE FOR THE YOUNG writers of the Harlem Renaissance was not all work and chronic poverty. There were also good times. Harlem of the 1920s was alive with music and theater. A keen eye might catch a glimpse of any number of celebrated African Americans strolling along Harlem avenues.

"There is another important aspect of Harlem of the Twenties," writes African-American playwright Lofton Mitchell, "and that was *joie de vivre*. There was a feeling, a spirit, a drive, a hope that black people had found the Promised Land."

A'Lelia Walker, the daughter of the famed Madame C.J. Walker, held a salon of writers, artists, and entertainers known as the "Dark Tower Tea Club" in her Harlem townhouse.

Though a student at Lincoln University, Hughes spent every free moment he could in the heart of Harlem. There, in Harlem, were his friends, black theater, and black music. There, in Harlem, he haunted the music halls and cabarets, living off of blues and jazz music. And, there, in Harlem, were the ordinary people, the black people who populated his poems and short stories.

One of the most popular gathering places for the young literati, the black intelligentsia, and noted entertainers was a Harlem townhouse on West 136th Street. It was one of several residences owned by A'Lelia Walker, the heiress to a fortune. A room in the well-appointed townhouse became the home of the "Dark Tower Tea Club," a gathering of writers and entertainers.

A'Lelia was a more than gracious hostess. And she was one of the wealthiest black women in the nation, if not the wealthiest. Her mother had been an anonymous washer woman until she invented a hair-straightening product for African-American women. Under the name Madame C.J. Walker, the ex-washer woman made millions of dollars producing products for the African-American beauty supply market.

"It was the period when the Negro was in vogue," Hughes recalled later.

It was an exciting time for all involved. All manner of African-American art flourished and captured the attention—and the much-needed dollars—of a more than curious white market. But it was the music that was the throbbing soul of the renaissance period, music that bellowed from the hot smoky interiors of nightclubs like the gangster-owned Cotton Club.

Though black entertainers lured wealthy, adventurous whites into the major Harlem nightspots, African Americans were barred by a "color line" that obstructed them, even there, in the Mecca of black culture.

Writer Chester Himes, famous for his series of Harlem detective novels, also recognized the irony of Harlem's existence. Himes observed that "most of the commercial enterprises—stores, bars, restaurants, theaters, etc.—and real estate are owned by white people.

"But it is the Mecca of the black people just the same. The air and the heat and the voices and the laughter, the atmosphere and the drama and the melodrama, are theirs. Theirs are the hopes, the schemes, the prayers and the protest. They are the managers, the clerks, the cleaners, they drive the taxis and the buses, they are the clients, the customers, the audience; they work it, but the white man owns it. So it is natural that the white man is concerned with their behavior; it's his property. But it is the black people's to enjoy. The black people have the past and the present, and they hope to have the future."

Harlem was more than a place to African Americans. It was a happening that somehow became symbolic of both the accomplishments and the failures of African Americans.

In a classic poem, "Esthete In Harlem," Hughes passionately expresses the highs and lows of life in his adopted home:

Strange,
That in this nigger place
I should meet life face to face,
When, for years, I had been seeking
Life in places gentler-speaking,
Until I came to this vile street
And found Life stepping on my feet!

W.E.B. Du Bois continued to state the social/political position of African Americans from his post as editor of *The Crisis*. The African American, wrote DuBois "would not Africanize America, for America has too much to teach the world and Africa. He would not bleach his Negro soul in a flood of white Americanism, for he knows that Negro blood has a message for the world. He simply wishes to make it possible for a man to be both a Negro and an American, without being cursed

Chester Himes was one of the youngest members of the Harlem Reniassance, just beginning his career in the 1930s and reaching maturity in the 1940s, but he was very outspoken about the fact that few Harlem businesses were owned by African Americans.

and spit upon by his fellows, without having the doors of opportunity closed roughly in his face."

It seemed, for a time that things were changing. The condition of the African American was on an upswing. Had they overcome? In 1925, Tuskegee Institute, reported only seventeen lynchings! It was an impressive decline in anti-Negro violence from a high of 115 reported in 1900. (Tuskegee, founded by Booker T. Washington, had kept meticulous records of anti-Negro violence since the turn of the century.)

Hughes was busy working on his first novel, somehow juggling his writing with his studies and trips to Harlem, which was still "heaven" for Hughes. He spent as much time there as he could.

In his senior year at Lincoln, Hughes won the Witter Bynner undergraduate prize for poetry. He was excited by the honor but was more concerned about finishing his studies and, as importantly, his novel.

Hughes graduated from Lincoln in 1929, prepared to take up full-time residence in Harlem. He was anxious to spend more time writing. He completed his novel shortly after graduation. The future seemed bright.

But, in October of 1929, the lives and futures of millions of Americans, white and black, were tragically changed forever. The nation's stock market crashed, and panic raged throughout the upper echelons of American finance. The nation was in the icy death-grip of the Great Depression.

African Americans suffered severely as the Depression forced vital industries to close their doors. Millions of Americans were out of work and were soon forced out of their homes.

The young writers of the Harlem Renaissance were not immune to the Depression and its side-effects. Once loyal, caring, and generous white patrons turned their backs and closed their pocketbooks to the "exotic" African-American writers.

Hughes' contemporary and close friend Arna Bontemps understood the rising lack of interest in Harlem on the part of once avid white fans. Bontemps candidly recalls, "The white intelligentsia's...involvement with the black artist appears to have been merely a part of their fascination with the exotic. Blacks represented the uninhibited man that they idealized. He was the noble savage, the carefree child of nature."

Hughes continued to have some success with his writings, though a misunderstanding with his wealthy white patron cut off a much-needed source of revenue. She had enjoyed his more "primitive" pieces; poems that captured the "hot, dark soul" of black America. She could not understand his need to turn his fine talent to more political, less enjoyable writing. The Depression only hastened Hughes' separation from his patron.

It was an emotional moment for Hughes. He was thankful for all his wealthy patron had done for him to that point. Without her assistance he might not have completed his college studies. And there were countless times he could recall when her generosity staved off starvation and provided him with shelter.

"Shortly poetry became bread," Hughes recalls, "prose shelter and raiment. Words turned into songs, plays, scenarios, articles, and stories. Literature is a big sea full of many fish. I let down my nets and pulled."

In 1930, Alfred A. Knopf published Hughes' first novel, *Not Without Laughter.* The novel was based on experiences and characters from Hughes' childhood days in Kansas. The book was an immediate success and was eventually translated into eight foreign languages: Spanish, Dutch, French, Italian, Japanese, Russian, Swedish, and Swiss.

Hughes was honored with the prestigious Harmon Award for literature in 1930. The award was sponsored by the Harmon Foundation, created by philanthropist William C. Harmon in December of 1926. A four-hundred-dollar cash prize accompanied the award. The money was, at the time, more important than the accolades that followed. The cash prize allowed Hughes to pay back rent, outstanding debts, and finance a trip to Haiti.

Two more books of poems by Langston Hughes were published in 1931. *Dear Lovely Death* was published by Troutbeck Press, and *The Negro Mother* was published by Golden Star Press.

Tragically, in August of 1931, The Dark Tower Tea Club lost its generous and cordial hostess. A'Lelia Walker died at age forty-six.

"It was really the end of the gay times of the New Negro era in Harlem," recalled Hughes in his autobiography. "That spring for me (and I guess, all of us) was the end of the Harlem Renaissance. We were no longer in vogue, anyway, we Negroes. Sophisticated New Yorkers turned to Noel Coward. Colored actors began to go hungry, publishers politely rejected new manuscripts, and patrons found other uses for their money.... The generous 1920s were over."

Vintage ❧ Classics

Stories by
Langston Hughes

The Ways of White Folks

Chapter Ten

A Writer's Life

THE HARLEM RENAISSANCE, the literary awakening of a people, ended. But Langston Hughes and other young writers like Zora Neale Hurston continued to write and live in Harlem.

In 1932, Hughes teamed with longtime friend Arna Bontemps in co-authoring a children's book, *Popo and Fifina, Children of Haiti*. Another children's book, *The Dream Keeper and Other Poems*, featuring Hughes' poems alone, was also published in 1932. The title poem reads, in part:

Although the interest of whites in black writers seemed to fade with the passing of the 1920s, the works of Langston Hughes continued to be published. His first collection of short stories, The Ways of White Folks, *was highly praised.*

Bring me all your dreams,
That I may wrap them
Away from the too-rough fingers
Of the world.

In June of 1932 a unique opportunity was presented to Langston Hughes. He was offered, along with twenty-two other African Americans, a trip to Russia to make a motion picture with the Meschrabpom Film Corporation. Hughes anxiously accepted, prepared to sate his thirst for travel. The group was housed in the New Moscow Hotel upon their arrival.

It was an important opportunity. The film, entitled *Black and White*, was to be an insightful look at the condition of race relations in the United States. To that point, meaningful portrayals of African Americans in Hollywood films had been sorely lacking. In the 1930s, commercial filmmaking was still in its infancy. Hughes saw this opportunity to really make a landmark contribution to the industry.

The Russian film was never completed. Hughes soon learned that the Russians knew very little about the complicated racial situation in America. The script could not be saved and the project was scrapped.

Hughes spent a year traveling in Russia before returning to Harlem. *The Ways of White Folks,* a collection of short stories by Langston Hughes, was published. Longtime friend and supporter Carl Van Vechten reviewed the book, writing, "Langston Hughes has now turned his attention to the short story and in this difficult form, at his best, immediately challenges comparison with such masters of the art as Katherine Mansfield and Chekhov."

Image was still of major concern to African Americans on Hughes' return to Harlem. The question of positive identity had yet to be fully resolved. And white, mainstream America seemed to shape and control the image of the African American, shallowly defining and degrading the race.

The mark of inferiority was the birthright of blacks as then defined by whites. And it had always been, it seemed, the intention of many white Americans to shackle the African American to that birthright.

"The entire history of the Negro in the United States," wrote E. Franklin Frazier, "has been to create in the Negro a feeling of racial inferiority..., his exclusion from the races of mankind."

Bert Williams, a popular African-American entertainer before and during the Harlem Renaissance, recalled the hideous stereotypes

In 1932, Langston Hughes teamed up with longtime friend Arna Bontemps (left) to write a children's book, Popo and Fifina, Children of Haiti. *In addition to books for young people,*

Bontemps wrote poetry and published several novels. He also anthologized the works of other writers. For a time he worked at Fisk University as the college librarian.

and their impact on black entertainers. "Black-faced white comedians," Williams said, "made themselves look as ridiculous as they could when portraying a 'darky' character. In their make-up they always had tremendously big red lips, and their costumes were frightfully exaggerated. The one fatal result of this to the colored performers was that they imitated the white performers in their make-up as 'darkies.' Nothing seemed more absurd than to see a colored man making himself ridiculous in order to portray himself."

There were African Americans who fought the grotesque pattern of stereotypes on America's stages and in American films. The great African-American singer/actor Paul Robeson had established himself as the premier African-American actor. A gifted dramatic and musical performer, Robeson made the transition from stage to film in the mid-1930s. He, like Hughes, was determined to show the depth and breadth of African-American art. Robeson, like many of the writers of the now dormant Harlem Renaissance, believed, "One of the great measures of a people is its culture, its artistic stature. Above all things, we boast that the only true artistic contributions of America are Negro in origin."

Hughes began writing plays in order to help to shape a more positive image of the African

American. On October 24, 1935, *Mulatto* opened on Broadway to begin the longest run for any play by an African American until Lorraine Hansberry's *A Raisin in the Sun* in the 1950s. (The first play by an African American to be produced on Broadway was Garland Anderson's *Appearances* in 1925.)

And in 1938, Hughes founded the Harlem Suitcase Theatre, a committed band of writers, actors, and actresses who were determined to keep black theater alive in Harlem.

The efforts of Hughes and other African-American communicators and image-makers in Harlem seemed futile, given the technical prowess of mainstream image-distorters. The caricature of the "shuffling darky" that had haunted blacks through America's theater stages and through commercial products from toothpaste to syrup, had not died away. The bug-eyed, wide-of-lip, insulting caricature had made the transition to film almost intact.

Hollywood was seemingly a part of the plot to prove African Americans inferior. In the late 1930s, Hollywood released the now classic film version of the Margaret Mitchell bestselling novel, *Gone With the Wind*. Whatever gains were made by African Americans in uplifting the collective image of the race was overshadowed by this film, which somehow reflected the national sentiment concerning blacks.

In the 1930s, there was a return to the old stereotypes of blacks in the American dramatic arts, particularly in Hollywood films such as Gone with the Wind. *Although Hattie McDaniel won*

an Academy Award for her performance in the film (the first black to win an Oscar), her role was that of Scarlett O'Hara's slave "Mammy," which she managed to carry off with dignity.

African Americans made major gains in the 1930s and early 1940s. Thurgood Marshall, a classmate of Langston's at Lincoln University, was now a practicing lawyer fighting civil rights court battles all the way to the United States Supreme Court. In 1940, Marshall argued and won his first case, *Chambers v. Florida,* before the Supreme Court.

African Americans like Jesse Owens were making history in the world of sports, while also battling against racism. In 1936, during the Berlin Olympic Games, held in Nazi Germany, Owens sprinted to gold-medal wins in the one hundred and two hundred meter dashes, also winning a gold medal and setting a new world record in the long jump. The leader of the host country for the Olympics, Adolf Hitler, stormed angrily out of the stadium to avoid shaking the hand of Jesse Owens. Hitler considered all black people as members of an inferior race. Ironically, white Americans cheered Owens' victories for the United States, while still denying his fellow African Americans basic human rights.

For African Americans the "self-evident" truths that "all men are created equal, that they are endowed by their Creator with certain inalienable rights..., life, liberty, and the pursuit of happiness..." were not so evident.

During this time there were angry young

Racism in the 1930s was most virulent in Nazi Germany, where Adolf Hitler proclaimed a master race of Aryans. When Jesse Owens won gold medals at the Berlin Olympics, Hitler stormed out of the stadium, enraged.

voices rising to challenge the system of racial oppression, among them writers like Richard Wright, based in Chicago, who echoed the philosophies and purposes of Hughes and most of the Harlem-based writers. Wright's first novel, *Native Son,* introduced the world to the angry, volatile soul of black America in the menacing form of Bigger Thomas.

Wright ignored the controversial attacks from whites *and* blacks and countered, "We write out of what life gives us in the form of experience. And there is a value in what we Negro writers say. Is it not clear to you that the American Negro is the only group in our nation that consistently and passionately raises the question of freedom? This is a service to America and to the world. More than this. The voice of the American Negro is rapidly becoming the most representative voice of America and of oppressed people anywhere in the world today."

In January of 1940, Hughes was making the final changes on the first volume of his autobiography, *The Big Sea.* It had only been fifteen years since the publication of his first collection of poems, *The Weary Blues.*

Hughes became popular as a poet and in demand. He visited schools throughout the country and, in October 1941, spoke at a special program at an all-black high school in

Angry young voices like that of Richard Wright, author of Native Son, *rose up in the 1940s, shocking the literary establishment with more realistic views of African-American life than had been published before.*

Sacramento, California.

On December 7, 1941, the Japanese attacked the United States naval installation at Pearl Harbor, Hawaii, and the country was thrust into World War II. On that fateful day, Dorie Miller, an African-American messman stationed aboard the *USS Arizona*, earned a place in American history for his heroic actions. At the height of the surprise attack, Miller carried a wounded officer to safety before manning one of the ship's machine guns. Though not trained as a combat machine-gunner (African Americans were considered unfit for combat, even though they have distinguished themselves in all of America's wars), Miller exchanged fire with attacking Japanese planes, shooting down four during the intense battle. He received the Navy Cross for his actions.

From May through August of 1943, a series of race riots erupted throughout the nation. For a tragic moment black and white Americans forgot the war in Europe and in the South Pacific and openly battled each other in the streets of America. Riots raged in Mobile, Alabama; Detroit, Michigan; Beaumont, Texas; and Harlem, New York.

Harlem was still home for Langston Hughes. The violence escalated as more and more African-American GIs returned from the war. And, like after World War I, black veterans of World War II found only unemployment and anti-black violence on their return home.

Hughes continued to write. And, in 1943, he received an honorary doctorate from his college alma mater, Lincoln University. It was also during the war years that Hughes introduced what would become his most beloved character, Jesse B. Simple. The character was featured in short, humorous sketches printed in the *Chicago Defender* newspaper. The character quickly became a folk hero and philosopher among readers of the popular column. The character became so real to the readers that letters began arriving at the paper addressed to "Mr. Jesse B. Simple."

Eugenia Collier, a Baltimore-based teacher and writer, observed: "In the panorama of Simple's Harlem certain characters stand out sharply. On one level they are believable individuals because we have all known people like them. Some of them change through the years, grow, mellow; others remain fairly well the same. On another level the Simple characters are something more than individuals.... The basic factor of Harlem is Blackness: the key dimension of Blackness is the response to white racism and its effects. Simple's friends adjust in their individual ways to the psychological and economic trap in which they are caught by reason of their Blackness in this America."

For Hughes, Jesse B. Simple was the embodiment of the Harlem he had grown to know and love. And his voice was its voice, questioning, probing, challenging. The humor hid a razor sharp wit that cut to the heart of the racial problem in America.

Simple was an ordinary man, a worker, much like the one featured in the Hughes poem "Black Workers," which appeared in the *The Crisis* magazine:

The bees work.
Their work is taken from them.
We are like the bees—
But it won't last
Forever.

THE BEST OF SIMPLE
LANGSTON HUGHES

AMERICAN CENTURY SERIES

It was during the 1940s that Langston Hughes created his most enduring and endearing character—that of Jessie B. Simple—in a series of sketches and stories written for the Chicago Defender.

Chapter Eleven

A Militant Past

.

WORLD WAR II ENDED in 1945 with the surrender of the Japanese. The world had entered a new era, an atomic era, with the dropping of the devastating atomic bomb on Nagasaki and Hiroshima. The war ended with a blast heard around the world!

The war ended with "democracy" the victor over tyranny and oppression, but the end of hostilities overseas did not mean the end of hostilities for African Americans at home in the United States. Returning GIs were met with violence and unemployment.

A. Philip Randolph expressed the feelings of

A Philip Randolph, here seen with black union members, succeeded in opening up employment opportunities for African Americans in the armaments industries during World War II.

African Americans, including Langston Hughes, when he declared, "A community is democratic only when the humblest and weakest person can enjoy the highest civil, economic, and social rights that the biggest and most powerful possess.... By fighting for their rights now, American Negroes are helping to make America a moral and spiritual arsenal of democracy."

Langston Hughes spent much of the mid-1940s traveling across the country in a beat-up old flivver. He read his poetry to thousands, telling his close friend Arna Bontemps for an *Ebony* magazine article: "My first [public appearance] was in Washington in 1924, so in twenty-two years I'd estimate from Mississippi to Moscow and Chicago to Shanghai [I've made] well over a thousand public appearances reading my poems."

Hughes guessed that he had read his most famous poem, "The Negro Speaks of Rivers," before over 500,000 people. "Although," he quipped, "I doubt if the Chinese understood it." By the end of 1946, Hughes had completed six cross-country tours reading his poetry.

Times were difficult for Hughes. He was barely breaking even with the small fees he earned from financially strapped colleges and selling copies of his books while on tour. In a March 16, 1948, letter to Arna Bontemps,

Hughes confessed, "I wish the rent/Was heaven sent." He was given a one-thousand-dollar "Arts and Letters" grant from the American Academy of Arts and Letters. The financial windfall eased his burdens for awhile. And, by August of 1949, Hughes had completed his first book featuring the popular Harlem philosopher, Jesse B. Simple. The work was fifty short chapters in length. The mid-1950s were a turbulent and volatile period in an America that had yet to shed its racist practices. African Americans were taking their struggle to the streets. They marched. They demanded. They picketed, boycotted, prayed. They vowed that they would "overcome."

Hughes, though known for his Harlem "dialect" poetry, had, throughout his career, revealed a more politically militant side in his poetry. Much of that poetry appeared in left-wing magazines like the *New Masses.*

Good Morning Revolution: Uncollected Writings of Social Protest, edited by Faith Berry (Hughes' biographer), focuses on the more militant writings by Langston Hughes. In the foreword to the work, Saunders Redding writes that "no poet caught with such sharp immediacy and intensity the humor and the pathos, the irony and the humiliation, the beauty and the bitterness of the experience of being Negro in America...." But Redding points out that people have too long ignored the fact that "Hughes was a revolutionary writer and poet."

Written in 1936, the opening lines of the poem "Good Morning, Revolution" express a more militant side of the black poet laureate:

Good morning, Revolution:
You're the very best friend
I ever had.
We gonna pal around together from now on.

And, in his poem "White Man," Hughes attacked job discrimination:

You're a White Man.
I'm a Negro.
You take all the best jobs
And leave us the garbage cans to empty and
The halls to clean....
Is your name spelled
C-A-P-I-T-A-L-I-S-T?

The angry, militant, anti-capitalist side of poet Langston Hughes did not go unnoticed by everyone. In March of 1953, Hughes and a number of prominent black and white Americans, including Paul Robeson and Jackie Robinson, were called before the Senate Judiciary Committee's Subcommittee on Internal Security, chaired by Senator Joseph

The late 1940s and the early 1950s became known as the "McCarthy Era" because of Senator Joseph McCarthy's investigations of priminent figures with liberal beliefs. Paul Robeson (above with Richard Wright) was one of those attacked.

McCarthy. Under the guise of defending America against the "communist menace," the committee indicted many innocent and patriotic Americans, blacks and whites.

Hughes was placed on McCarthy's "hit list" of so-called "un-American" authors. Hughes' books were banned in libraries throughout the world; the lecture bureau that scheduled reading and speaking engagements for Hughes quickly dropped the once popular writer.

Langston Hughes would state his case before the McCarthy committee in a statement that also appeared in *The Crisis* magazine.

> I am not now and never have been a member of the Communist party.... In my youth, faced with the problems of both poverty and color, and penniless at the beginning of the depression, I was strongly attracted by some of the promises of communism, but always with the reservations, among others, of a creative writer wishing to preserve my own freedom of action and expression, and as an American Negro desiring full integration into our body politic. These two reservations, particularly (since I could never accept the totalitarian regimentation of the artist nor the Communist theory of a Negro state for the Black Belt) were among other reasons why I never contemplated joining the Communist party, although various aspects of Communist inter-

ests were for some years reflected in the emotional content of my writing.

Hughes expressed the attitudes of most African Americans, reaffirming their loyalty and belief in American democracy at a time when they, black people, had a right to question America's loyalty to them, citizens who had given a great deal in the defense of their country.

In his book, *The First Book of Negroes,* Hughes wrote:

Our country has many problems still to solve, but America is young, big, strong, and beautiful. And we are trying very hard to be, as the flag says, "one nation, indivisible, with liberty and justice for all." Here people are free to vote and work out their problems. In some countries people are governed by rulers, and ordinary folks can't do a thing about it. But here all of us are a part of a democracy. By taking an interest in our government, and by treating our neighbors as we would like to be treated, each one of us can help make our country the most wonderful country in the world.

Hughes was a believer in the possibilities offered by American democracy when properly implemented to include all of its citizens under its umbrella of protection and prosperity.

On May 17, 1954, the United States Supreme Court reached a decision in the civil rights case of *Oliver Brown v. the Board of Education of Topeka*. The decision staggered entrenched racists in the South who had traditionally ignored federal laws prohibiting racial discrimination in employment, transportation, and education. The landmark case had been argued before the court by former Hughes classmate Thurgood Marshall. Hughes could not help but recall the difficulty he had experienced in convincing Marshall to join him in his crusade to integrate the all-white faculty of Lincoln University. They had both come a long way in the face of racial oppression.

In expressing the court's decision Chief Justice Earl B. Warren of the United States Supreme Court said:

> We cannot turn the clock back to 1868 when the [Fourteenth] Amendment was adopted, or even to 1896, when *Plessy v. Ferguson* was written.... We come then to the question presented: Does segregation of children in public schools solely on the basis of race, even though the physical facilities and other tangible factors may be equal, deprive the children of the minority group of equal educa-

The NAACP, under the guidance of Roy Wilkins, Walter White, and Thurgood Marshall, made a major breakthrough in 1954 by pressing the case of Brown v. the Board of Education of Topeka *before the U.S. Supreme Court.*

tional opportunities? We believe that it does.

On January 9, 1957, Langston Hughes completed his second book of short sketches featuring the character, Jesse B. Simple, *Simple Stakes a Claim.* That same year Hughes was honored with the Manhattan Man of the Year plaque from the New York Omegas.

Hughes' Jesse B. Simple became an internationally known character. In early 1958, Hughes was introduced to famous French mime Marcel Marceau by the writer who was translating the Hughes work, *Simply Heavenly,* into French. And in December 1959, the American version of *Simply Heavenly* aired on television as part of the Play-of-the-Week series. Noted singer/actor/dancer Oscar Brown, Jr., starred as Jesse B. Simple.

Langston Hughes, a permanent resident of Harlem, continued to write poetry and plays and to translate the poetry of French and Spanish writers until his untimely death in May of 1967.

A full-page Hughes memorial appeared in *Negro Digest*, in June 1967:

IN MEMORIAM
LANGSTON HUGHES
1902-1967
...And when he fell in whirlwind, he went down

As when a lordly cedar, green with boughs,
Goes down with a great shout upon the hills,
And leaves a lonesome place against the sky...
    —From "Lincoln, the Man of the People"
                by Edwin Markham

African-American writer/critic John Henrik Clarke praised Hughes in his introduction to *Harlem: From the Soul of Black America,* writing, "Langston Hughes was more than the Poet Laureate of Harlem. Of all the black writers, he has conveyed the most genuine feeling of love and concern for the people of this community. His greatest contribution to the literature of Harlem, and to Afro-American literature in general, is the urban folk hero, Jesse B. Simple."

And Arthur P. Davis, observed, "From the very beginning of his literary career, he was determined to forge his art, not of the second-hand material which came from books, not of fads dictated by a demanding patron, but out of the stuff of human experience as he saw it."

Faith Berry, Hughes' biographer, captured the essence of Langston Hughes and his work, writing, "In order to satisfy his public, his critics, his publishers, and himself, he faced an ongoing inner struggle between what he wanted to write and what his audience expected him to write, between his public image and private self, between his performance and his integrity."

Thankfully, for fans throughout the world, Langston Hughes saw himself as a "propaganda or a protest writer," declaring, "I write about what I know best, and being a Negro in this country is tied up with difficulties that cause one to protest naturally. I am writing about human beings and situations that I know and experience, and therefore it is only incidentally protest—protest in that it grows out of a live situation."

The "live" situation was, and had always been, ongoing discrimination against African Americans. That racially based discrimination had denied African Americans their rightful share of the American Dream. In one of his most noted poems, Langston Hughes asked:

What happens to a dream deferred?
Does it dry up
like a raisin in the sun?
...Or does it explode?

INDEX

PICTURE CREDITS

Alain Locke Papers, Moorland-Spingarn Research Center, Howard University: 121; A. Philip Randolph Institute: 67; Archives of the University of Massachusetts at Amherst: 11, 19; Culver Pictures: 94, 167; Duncan P. Scheidt: 78; Eddie Brandt Saturday Matinee: 162–163; Florida State Archives: 41, 81; Frank Driggs Collection: 177; Frank Leslie's Illustrated Weekly: 32–33; Griffith J. Davies: 158–159; Indiana Historical Society: 144; Langston Hughes Estate: 21, 24, 55, 62, 119, 133; Library of Congress: 17, 39, 51, 126, 137, 172, 181; Lincoln University: 130–131; National Archives: 98–99; New York Public Library, Astor, Lenox and Tilden Foundation: 8, 75, 103, 110, 123, 149; Oberlin College Library: 29; Ohio Historical Society: 46; Players International Archives: 27, 43, 85, 115, 165; Marianne Greenwood: 93; The Schomburg Center for Research of Black Culture, New York Public Library, Astor, Lenox and Tilden Foundation: 15, 59, 71, 105; Theater Collection, Museum of the City of New York: 89; Van Der Zee: 101.

Melrose Square Publishing has made every effort to reach the copyright holders of all the photographs reproduced in this book.